Chasing CHASE

"The Chase Series"

MEKO

ISBN-13: 9780615997353
Library of Congress Control Number: 2014938584
Eagle Life Publications, Dallas, TX

CHAPTER 1
"REALLY?"

Howling screams of excruciating pain is all that I can hear as I open the door to my three-story home. Shocked to see my face, Chad lowers his pistol and yells at me. "Chase, why are you here? What in the hell are you doing here?"

"Because I live here—that's why! What are you doing here, and where's Lamar?" I yell back with a look of confusion on my face. That instantly turns into anger after I walk farther into my foyer, and see Ken and some guy that I've never seen before standing talking.

"What are y'all doing in my house? And where in the hell is Lamar? And I know that y'all can hear all of that moaning and groaning, who is that?" I ask while nervously wondering why the music is so loud, and completely shocked that Lamar would have these dudes inside of our home like this.

When he's the main one who would never even allow our own family members to just roam around our place, let alone strangers. But I guess the sounds of someone being in excruciating pain should be my biggest concern right now.

1

"I can't let you go down there, Chase!"
Chad says while stepping in front of me to block my attempt to go down my own entryway steps.
"Wait here and let me go and get Lamar for you!"
"This is my house, and I can go wherever I want to go! So excuse me because I'm going down those steps regardless of what you say!"
"CJ, don't do this!"
He continues to block me while trying to explain.
"You have to stand right here and let me go and get him for you, because it's some serious shit going on right now, and you shouldn't be here!"
Looking even more serious as he releases the grip that he has on my arm, then he stares at me for a second and then turn around to go and get Lamar for me.
And I know the best thing for me to do right now would probably be to just stand here and wait for him to return like he asked me to. But it's extremely difficult to just stand here and wait for him when I keep hearing the loud and consistent sounds of moaning and groaning like someone's in pain.
So almost immediately after he turns his back to go and inform Lamar of my presence, I trail behind him. Taking baby steps until I am close enough to get a clear view of Lamar living out more of his gangster fantasies right here in our home of all places.
"Oh my God! What are you doing down here, Lamar?"
I scream while bursting into tears after seeing Tony tied to a chair and drenched in blood.
"Tony's like family!"
"You hear that, you piece of shit?"
Lamar raves, then aims his gun directly at Tony's right shoulder, and then pulls the trigger. Blasting a single shot into his flesh after hearing me say that he's like family.

2

"I guess family can't wait to rape family these days, huh," he fallaciously continues to yell at him. "See how she feels about you, motherfucka!"

Crippling him even more, Lamar squeezes the trigger yet again, but it's now aimed at his left shoulder.

Then out of nowhere, he turns around to Chad with a look of rage in his eyes and says.

"So it's that easy for her to get past you to come down here and see this shit, Chad?"

Now he tells him to take me back upstairs, while looking over me like I'm not here.

So I interrupt him. "I'm not going anywhere, Lamar, and why won't you look at me? Why are you doing this to Tony?"

And after all of these years of being with Lamar, I've never seen him like this before. His whole demeanor has my body trembling all over, and even more so now after seeing how he has Tony tied up and bleeding from both knees, both feet, both hands, both arms, and now both shoulders. And he's still alive.

But now he says to me.

"Look over there on that table and see all of the info that I got on how far our loyal family member right here was about to go to disrespect this motherfucking house!"

Still never making any direct eye contact with me, he continues to bark with the rage of an agitated bull.

"Now this house is where he's going to do what he had planned for us to do here tonight, if his little plan would have worked out!"

"What are you talking about?"

I cry out even more. "I just don't understand!"

"I'm talking about how this bitch made ass fool came over here to set me, you, and the girls up to be robbed, raped, and killed tonight!" He yells at me as the veins in his neck grow as big as fishing worms, like they do every time he gets really angry.

3

"He's got some traitors on their way over here right now to handle that shit for him, but I got a surprise waiting for their asses when they get here!"

Boom, boom, boom!

Sounds of commotion all of a sudden ring out at the top of the steps, and now sweat begins to pour from my forehead. And my palms begin to feel like I've been playing in water while I now understand, and completely realize that I really don't need to be here right now.

But it's too late to leave now, because I can hear the gunshots ringing out upstairs. So I eagerly begin to scatter my footsteps along with everyone else's at this point because I don't want to be robbed, raped, or killed tonight.

And now I jump to my feet after rolling damn near off the couch and onto the floor after hearing the loud knocking sounds at my front door that has awakened me from this terrible nightmare. — After I'd fallen asleep while waiting on Rajon to stop by to pick up the shirts that Indira had left in the trunk of my car.

Rajon's loud knocking scared the hell out of me, right in the middle of me thinking that I was about to die or something—so I run to the door to open the flap to see who it is.

And just as I figured, it's Rajon. Standing on my front porch looking stupid, and knocking like he's the damn police.

I guess he figured that the louder he knocked, the better it would be. Instead of simply using the doorbell.

"Damn, Rajon!" I yell at him as soon as I open the door.

"Why in the hell are you beating on my door like you're the police? Come on in here and have a seat while I run to the bathroom!"

"All right," he says.

"I've been knocking for a long time, but I thought that you were sleep, so I was trying to wake you up!"

"I did fall asleep waiting for you to get here, but I'm sure that I would have probably heard the doorbell if you would have tried to ring it! But I'm glad that you woke me up anyway, because I was having one of the worst dreams that I've had in a long time. I'm still trembling like I'm about to be shot or raped or something."

I now close the front door and run to the bathroom to relieve myself, and to gather my thoughts.

And as I return to the living room to finish with Rajon, and to hopefully go back to sleep—but sleep peacefully this time. I continue on.

"Okay, Rajon, let me grab my keys. Then we can head to the car now that I don't have to worry about pissing on myself."

"Cool."

He now asks about my dream while at the same time making it painfully obvious that my breasts would be a better subject for him right now.

"CJ, what was your dream about?" He asks with his eyes planted directly onto my chest—so much so that I have to place my hands over my breasts when we make it to my car.

And after handing him the shirts, he's still staring at me like he doesn't care if I see him or not. Even though he knows that Indira is my friend, and I'm even the one who hooked them up. But just as sure as hell is hot, his eyes are glued to my breasts so much that I say.

"Don't worry about my dream Rajon! Do you need anything else? While you're out here looking at my chest like you done lost your damn mind!"

"Nope," he says.

"This is it."

"Okay, well, tell Indira to call me when you get home."

"All right." He says while still looking at me smiling like he just took a mental picture of my breasts for his memory.

And sadly enough, he knows just as well as I do that I can't just go back inside and call Indira and tell her that her man was just over here eyeballing me like he wanted to be breast-fed.

I already know better than to call her with that kind of information after seeing her reaction to Sky, when we were at Adrian's baby shower before she gave birth to the twins.

My best friend, Sky, went to Indira and told her that she saw Rajon all hugged up with some chick at the theater. And she just wanted to tell her about it because she thought that it was really foul of him to be out here cuddling and kissing on another woman as if he was single.

And while a lot of women would have thanked her and taken the information for what it was worth. Indira made a comment that had us all wanting to beat her ass that day.

She literally said. "Okay, Sky, so now here you go telling me some shit about Rajon. — I mean what? You want to fuck him too, I see you must want a piece of the action too, huh?"

And I couldn't believe that she'd said that to her when Sky was only trying to look out for her well-being as her friend.

But Sky dropped everything that she was doing and yelled at her like she wanted to strangle her.

She yelled. "Look, bitch, I was just telling your stupid ass that Rajon was up to no good and shit! But you can best believe that you don't ever have to worry about me coming back telling your dumb ass nothing else!"

And we all agreed with Sky and understood why she was feeling like she wanted to rip her head off right then and there. And now that I think about it, we probably should have just let Sky beat her ass for acting like that. But it would have been pointless because we all know that Indira is in over her head now that she's with Rajon, anyway.

She told me that she liked him when I had first brought his name up to her, before I even thought about introducing them.

But I figured that after I'd ran everything down to her, she would eventually adapt to what I was telling her about him and his lifestyle.

But Indira doesn't listen to me or anyone else when it comes to connecting with a man, and that's cool because she's grown and free to do as she pleases.

However, in this situation she should have listened because she could have had Rajon exactly where she needs for him to be right now, if she weren't so damn stubborn.

I tried to tell her that nobody can really change a person, they must first want to change themselves, and Rajon was ready to change himself. — But it seems like since they've gotten together, she's made him worse instead of better.

And honestly, sometimes I think that he would have actually turned out to be a better person if I hadn't introduced him to her. And I've personally told her that, I mean she's my girl and everything, but she's got some serious issues when it comes to men.

And that's why I know that I'll be keeping this little information about Rajon staring at my chest to myself, because she's not going to believe me anyway. And that's why the distance between us will continue to be like it is, because Indira can and will make a person so mad that she'll have you wanting to knock her ass out every time you see her.

But sometimes I believe that not even she can believe some of the things that she does, or even allow to come out of her mouth. I told her that somewhere deep down within herself, I think that she can see that sometimes her notions about things are a little wild and crazy.

And that's why she doesn't take certain comments that are made about her to heart, because she knows that she's got some unusual issues going on inside of that brain of hers. - So believe me when I say that we've all had our ups and downs with Indira about how she sees things. But as a friend who has stuck with her throughout the thick and the thin. I can say that she can be trusted and will keep her word to me when it counts the most, regardless of her flaws. And that's whether it's dealing with some real business issues, or handling some personal street business.

I know that I can always depend on Indira when I need her without any questions asked, just as long as a man doesn't get into her mental space too much when the trust factor is in question.

She's proven to me more than once that she would rather get hurt than to betray me when it comes to her loyalty of being a friend to me. — And since it's becoming damn near impossible to find friends like that nowadays, we both just try to bond as much as we can and work with what we have in trusting each other as friends through whatever we go through.

But my closest and dearest friend is Sky, who's more like a sister to me, and she's totally different from Indira.

Sky has a boyfriend also, but their relationship is also a lot different because she's dating Chad, who I must say is perfect for her. He's baldheaded with a beard; tall, dark, and handsome.

Chad is the kind of fine that will make you haul off and punch a bitch in her face just for looking at him for too long.

That's why when they first met, she made sure that she locked in on him as soon as she found out that he was attending the same event that we were attending.

And now that she has him, she's still doing whatever she has to do to keep him and herself happy. She cooks often and keeps herself looking good by going hard at the gym every Tuesday and Thursday, and this is while maintaining a clean house and being in school full-time. And my girl still finds the time to spin with her kids and his kids, while making sure that all of their bills and businesses are kept current.

And from what I hear, she's been topping him off real good sexually in the bedroom, and wherever else that he would want it. And whenever he wants it.

Unless he doesn't deserve it, but even then she still may give it to him and just make him pay for it by way of cash later for her emotional troubles.

And that is exactly the way that I've influenced her to be, instead of getting mad over small stuff that can be fixed with honest communication, and money.

And there are only three other women whom I associate with on a regular basis, and they are; Adrian, Rayci, and Kris.

Adrian is married to Paul, and Rayci is married to Markus. And I met Kris through her boyfriend Chris, who is my closest male best friend.

I love Chris and have known him for many years, he's like my big brother. And usually any girlfriend of Chris's, somehow ends up becoming a girlfriend of mine.

So among the six of us, there's a variety of relationships and drama that comes along with the territory of being the so-called 'first ladies' in our men's lives.

We've all had our ups and downs with all types of drama, but we just play the hands that are dealt to us in this life. And try our best to live it to the fullest extent of our being.

CHAPTER 2
"MEMORY LANE"

S ky and I meet up to go and get something to eat and to have a drink, but we decide not to take both cars. So we end up taking my car back home so that I can get in with her.

But when we get to my house we go inside to roll a blunt; because that's just how we get down sometimes when we're together.

And we love going to this place called BJ's to eat and to drink, but we enjoy it a lot more when we arrive high and already a tad bit tipsy.

So while at my house sitting on the sofa and passing the blunt back and forth, we begin to reminisce about when she and Chad first got together. And how she was on a mission to lock him in as her man no matter what.

I told her that before any of us could get to his fine bowlegged ass, she made sure that she let us all know that she was going to eventually end up sleeping with him regardless of who got his number that night. So there was no need for any of us to even show him any interest because she wasn't going to back away from him under any circumstances.

"You guys have been kicking it tough for about three years now, right?"

"Yep," she answers. "Three years and six months!"

Now beaming with a huge smile on her face, showing me that he's still on top of his job of keeping her happy.

"I see that he's got you over here still smiling like you've got some sort of overactive smiling disorder!"

While laughing, I add. "And I'm loving it, too, because you really don't have to worry about a lot of bullshit when it comes to Chad."

"I really don't, CJ, but you know that it wasn't always like this though. Good thing everything has worked itself out, and we're straight now in all areas. Especially in our sex life. Girl, I'm so glad that I came to you about what I should do to try to fuck him until I saw some actions!"

"Really, what happened?"

"Nothing in particular, it's just that you know that things were a little shaky for us during our first year or so. But now within the past two years, everything that you were telling me to do has been working on every level. I mean now I've been doing all kinds of freaky stuff on my own without even thinking about it, and he loves it. Everything from letting him watch me pleasure myself, to me pleasuring him without boundaries. Especially since there's no outside interferences as far as other women are concerned, everything really is all good with us."

And as we continue our slow puff-puff-pass rotation, things begin to get a little more interesting as she continues to talk about how much more they have been exploring each other sexually.

And while I sit listening, I can remember how she would call me at three o'clock in the morning for dick-sucking tips to wake him up to— instead of her usual duck and suck that she would give him every now and then.

11

She says that she would call me because she wanted to spice things up, so that he would have something good to think about when he got up to start his day. — So I always gave her my most honest advice on whatever it was that she wanted to know sexually, no matter what it was.

Sky is like my sister, and just like she tells me about her and Chad, I can't keep some of the things that Lamar and I do to each other to myself either.

So she and I will just have to be an exception to the rule when it comes to keeping quiet about how good our men are in bed. — Because we share stories all the time, but she's definitely the one and only person whom I talk to as far as giving out any real details. Aside from giving advice.

Lamar doesn't have a bald head like Chad does, but he does have those sexy brown eyes and perfect waves with a goatee. Along with his hard sexy frame and dark caramel skin; he had me wanting to have sex with him at first sight, but I didn't.

And I'm so thankful that I had evolved to a mature enough level in my life that I wanted to make him my friend first before anything else. And since he was already financially walking a lot taller than everyone else that he hung out with, including Chad.

I knew that I couldn't just jump headfirst into anything with him due to his status alone—so I did things to make him work hard to even get a date with me.

But then after a lot of flirting, and me purposely baiting him.

I eventually managed to get his full attention on me and only me, and it led to us becoming a very exuberant couple that did things with each other that we've never done with anyone else.

"You and Lamar would be the perfect couple if y'all didn't fight all the time about his hustle."

Sky says. "But I understand what you've been saying about him letting that street life go now while he's financially able to do what he wants to do by choice, before the police comes in and do whatever they want to do to him by force."

"That's all that I be trying to tell him, and that's just smart thinking. I mean I wish nothing bad to come his way, but what makes him so different from everybody else is that he doesn't understand that his reality is just his reality. And I just want for him to face reality and see when enough is enough, but girl. Lamar just has a lot of things all together that he just needs to work on right now before we can go any further with our relationship."

Opening up a little more, I tell her.

"I honestly think that we would make a perfect couple, too, if he would just work on a few of his problems first. Because one time he told me that he had a dream that he'd cut out the belly of some dude and filled him with vodka. Then he went and found the guy's daddy and made him drink the vodka from his dead son's belly just for producing him. And he did it all because the guy had disrespected me, and nobody disrespects his woman and gets to live another day. Now you know that his ass is insane in the membrane for even having such a dream."

I now pause for a moment to think about how often his mind used to venture off into dark places like that. And how he would never acknowledge it as a problem to try and fix it.

"Chad told me that Lamar is off the chain when he's mad, but it takes a lot to get him mad."

Sky tells me of what she's heard from Chad, who's also seen Lamar upset from being around him for so long.

And he'll probably agree with me when I say that it's never a pleasant time for anyone when Lamar is really upset.

"Yeah, it does take a lot to get him upset, but all hell breaks loose when he does get there. Anyway, I'm ready to go because we were only supposed to come here to drop off my car before heading to the restaurant."

13

"I was just thinking the same thing after I looked at the time, but why is it that every time we start talking about our lives, time starts moving so fast all of a sudden?"

"I don't know, but I'm ready to go whenever you are, because I'm hungry now."

"Me, too. So let's go."

CHAPTER 3
"UPS AND DOWNS"

After leaving my house, Sky heads toward the restaurant and says. "Earlier, when we were talking about that game night/fight party at my house. Do you remember how Indira came running into the kitchen to tell us that Tyriq had just got shot at that club?"

"How can I forget?"

I begin to shake my head. "My jaw dropped when they showed where he and his friend had been shot and killed."

"Mine, too, CJ. I couldn't believe it. But I knew that something would eventually happen to him one day if he didn't slow his roll."

She says, "I felt bad about that whole situation because it was just sad what Angie had to go through."

"Same here. But a few days after everything had settled down, I went over there to spend some time with Angie. And it really was hard to see her go through that because you know she was out here doing her thing way before we were, but she dropped the ball somewhere along the way after getting with Tyriq."

"I mean she taught me early on how to get out here and get my own money, and then she schooled me on how to handle these men out here without getting hurt. I literally watched her make money and handle herself like a man, but in a womanly manner to get whatever she wanted. Until she started tripping— remember how I used to try to mimic her every move like she was my hero? Until she let me down when she got with Tyriq."

"Yes, your ass used to follow her around like you were her little puppy!"

"I sure did, and I'm not ashamed of it because she was a winner, but that was a long time ago. These are different days and times now, so things have definitely changed, and I knew that losing Tyriq was going to hit her hard. I mean I've never lost a baby daddy before, so I really didn't know how to come at her with that one. I kept asking myself what to say to a woman who seemingly lived her life strictly for her man, who'd just been murdered. Because I know that Angie knew Christ and everything like that, but it seemed like Tyriq came first over everybody, including God. One day we even got into a big argument because of how she was acting like he was the Almighty and ruled over everything. So I already knew that his death was going to take her even lower than she was, but thankfully she seems to always be so much happier now that he's not in her life."

"Yeah," Sky says, "I heard that she's way happier now that he's gone."

"She is, and I know that it's been a few years now since that happened. But I saw her about two weeks ago, and we talked for a long time about how good it was to still see her not bruised from him hitting her all the time. She said that no matter what she did back then, she just couldn't get away from him or his beatings when it came to her trying to leave him. So after a while she just gave up on even trying to leave, but now she says

16

that she can see how big of a mistake that was when she should have just put it in the Lord's hands and really just left him. Because Tyriq wasn't right, and now that he's gone, she can see better than ever that he was never good for her or anyone else around him. She told me that she doesn't know how she fell so in love with him like she did, but now she and her kids are happy. And I'm just glad to see that she's finally getting her life back together after being freed from all of that. She was left broke, homeless, and in so much debt after his funeral. Because Sharday had gotten just about everything that belonged to Tyriq, instead of her and those kids. Remember him and Sharday had gotten married when they were twenty-one years old, but then they broke up by the time they turned twenty-two. And they never officially got a divorce, so as his wife, Sharday could have even tried to keep Angie away from the funeral as much as they used to fight over him. And you know that would have been right up Sharday's alley to keep her away from his funeral, but she knew not to try anything that stupid when they both have kids by him."

"My thing is why would Angie drag her feet as far as making sure that Tyriq had all of that information straightened out before they even moved in together?"

Sky shouts. "She should have been checking all paperwork for everybody and for everything, and made whatever changes that needed to be made to make sure that her name was on whatever it was that she could afford to pay for on her own! Like you said, Angie was out here way before we were, so she knows better!"

She says. "But she just let Tyriq come in and bring her all the way down. I honestly thought that she would die before he would, judging by the way he used to disfigure her face. She don't even look the same anymore, even to this day. She's cute, but she still don't look like she used to. But I'm glad that she's changed her life because she should have been practicing what she preached and jumped that ship a long time ago."

Sky now adds that although she and Chad are going pretty strong, and she's got him almost exactly where she wants him to be.

She says that she'll never just overlook even the little things when she's feeling like something isn't right between them.

And I agree with her because I believe that communication is the key to all strong relationships.

Now, Sky's cell phone starts to ring.

"What's up, girl?" She answers after recognizing the number from the caller ID.

"Chase and I are headed to BJ's to get something to eat. Do you want to meet us there?"

She excitedly asks whomever is on the other end, knowing that we will quickly turn this night into a club-hopping ladies' night out.

"Okay, since you're already dressed, just meet us there in a minute!" She now hangs up and connects her phone to the phone charger.

"Who was that?"

"Eshia," she answers.

"She was supposed to stop by my place later, but she's just going to meet us at BJ's instead. You know that's Chad's sister, so I have to keep her close."

Now laughing in a really weird and sneaky way she says. "I try to keep all of his people close, and since Eshia's been calling and trying to hang out with me lately. I'm going to follow suit and go ahead and do my sister-in-law thing with her."

She says, "But tonight I think the three of us should head over to the pool hall and get a game going after we eat and have these drinks. Because if my memory serves me right, Chad and Lamar are supposed to be meeting up there tonight."

Frowning, I snarl at her. "I don't want to go anywhere they're going to be so that Lamar can watch my every move!"

"Girl, please!"

She shouts sarcastically. "Lamar is watching your every move anyway, so we can just leave that conversation right here where it's at. He hasn't moved on and neither have you, so I don't know why you're fronting and acting like you don't want to see him."

"I don't know what I want, but being around him while I'm trying to figure it out won't be making things any easier for me. So I don't want to be hanging out with him like everything is cool with us when we haven't made any real changes yet. So fronting or no fronting, I'd rather just go to that jazz spot downtown and hear their live band tonight. Versus going there." I parry because there's truth in what she's saying, and that's a big reason why I need to run in the opposite direction of him.

At least until I can figure out how much of him am I willing to settle for, since I clearly can't have what I want.

"How about if we just go on to BJ's like we're doing, and then decide from there what we're going to do next?"

"That's cool, Sky, but now I'm thinking that I probably should have just drove my own car after all. Because y'all will be going to the pool hall minus one if that's where our final destination is leaning toward being for tonight, for real."

"No you shouldn't have driven your car because we don't need both cars, and we don't have to end up with them. And I'm not turning around, so we'll just have to go to the jazz spot since you're acting all vulnerable and whatnot, because I can see Chad when I get home."

She says, "I just can't believe that you're acting like this when I know that you miss him."

"I sure do miss him, you're damn right about that! But that doesn't mean that I should be in his presence right now, because

I'm serious about walking away from him to protect me and my girls. Even if it hurts my heart, I'm just going to keep my distance until I know that I'm strong enough to see him without falling for his charm again."

"I understand, I just miss how much fun we all have when we get together that's all. But we have plenty of time to get together with them after y'all figure it all out, so let's just rock out however you want to tonight."

"Okay, cool."

CHAPTER 4
"LOVE ME ANYWAY"

"Good evening, ladies. Right this way."
Ming, the nice Asian lady who's always here when we sometimes meet here for lunch, and for our business meetings. Asks us to follow her.
"Oh, Ming, we want to sit at the bar this time."
I stop her as she walks us in the opposite direction of the bar.
"So sorry, Chase. I thought you want to sit with Mr. Mar in your reserved area on the patio."
"Sit with who?"
I shout while turning around to look at Sky, now thinking that she set me up. Knowing that I was trying to avoid Lamar tonight.
"CJ, on my momma, I didn't know that Lamar was going to be here! Earlier, I told Chad that we were thinking about coming to BJ's, but he didn't say anything about coming here or telling Lamar! I promise I didn't know Lamar would be here!"
She says while looking just as surprised as I am to hear Ming say that Mr. Mar has reserved a section already. Because we both immediately know who she's talking about when she said Mr. Mar, because everyone here at BJ's calls Lamar that.

"Hey baby, what up?" Chad says while creeping in from behind Sky, and grabbing her and pulling her close to him for a hug.

"Chad, why didn't you tell me that you and Lamar were going to be here tonight?"

"I didn't know that we were coming here until you said that you and CJ were having a drink up here. Lamar was sitting right beside me at the time, and he heard us talking. So when he asked, I told him that you and CJ might be stopping in here tonight. But I didn't know that he was going to put somebody on getting reservations so that we could end up with y'all before I even hung up the phone. Why? Y'all don't want to kick it with us or something?" He says while throwing his hands in the air and starts smiling.

"We do want to kick it with y'all but it's just not a good time right now for Chase and Lamar to be here together like this. And I don't want her to think that I had something to do with him being here, when I know that she wants her space away from him right now."

"Here you go, Chase." Chad says while handing me a rectangular black box while Sky is talking.

"What's this?" I utter while reaching for the box to open it.

"Oh my God." Is all that I can say to myself after seeing the gorgeous bracelet that Lamar has apparently gave to Chad to give to me.

"Chad, I seriously don't even feel like all of this tonight for real, and why do I always have to get an expensive ass gift when he knows that he's fucked up? Why don't he just get his shit together if he really wants me, instead of always throwing jewels and money at me all the time?"

"I don't know."

Still smiling, he says. "I'm just doing what he asked me to do."

"Yeah, I'm sure you are." I digress. "But I guess I'm kind of flattered."

22

I now pause for a second because I can already begin to feel myself quickly starting to renege on my word of staying away from him.

I can clearly see how this night is about to go if he's missing me like I think he is, because it's been almost a month since we've been together sexually. And I'm willing to have a sex session with him one last time that will hopefully last me until I can figure something else out. But this is the very reason why I've been trying to avoid seeing him, so that this wouldn't happen— but I'm here now. And I'm horny, so I'm just going to have to deal with the consequences of him taking whatever happens between us tonight too seriously later. Because I think it's sweet how he's placed a note inside of the box that says.

I know, I know, I know. But I Love Chasing Jordan.
Always, baby.

And while I know it's going to cause problems in the end, because I truly am not ready to get back with him yet. But he's just somehow going to have to accept my decision at some point.

"Come on, Chase! Let's just head to the patio because I'm hungry!"

Sky says as Eshia now walks up to us and immediately takes Chad's glass from his hand and drink from it.

"And since Lamar is presenting you with gifts and all of this love, we might as well go ahead and make our way to the patio where he is and show our appreciation," she says.

"Don't you think so?"

"What is it exactly that you appreciate though, Sky?" I ask while laughing because she only wants to stay here because Chad has her all discombobulated from hugging and kissing on her so much.

"I appreciate this food that I'm about to be eating as soon as we make it out here to this patio, so come on!"

Needing no time to be convinced to follow her, I walk behind her and onto the patio where the tables are already filled with food and alcohol for everyone who came with him and me to enjoy.

And the moment Lamar and I lay eyes on each other, I know that I won't be leaving anytime soon. So I walk over to embrace him with our usual hug and kiss that we always give when we see each other.

"I appreciate everything that you've done tonight, Lamar. But why don't you ever give me the space that I ask for during times like this?"

"Because I just can't, Chase. I can't help it. You didn't answer or return either of my calls the two times that I called you, so I figured I'd show you that I was thinking about you by buying you dinner after I heard that you would be here."

"Well, what about this bracelet? You know that I love it and everything like that, but why do I always have to get some kind of extravagant-ass gift like it's going to make up for what's going on with us?"

He immediately pulls me closer to him and says.

"Baby, I don't want to argue or get you all worked up tonight. I just want to spend some time with you and do something nice for you—that's all. And CJ, I know that you've heard all of this before, but things are going to be different this time."

He continues on while I close my eyes so that I don't have to look at him spill the same crap that he always spill on me when he's trying to gear my mind away from his mess.

But it's a good thing that I fall for what I want to fall for because tonight I need some loving just as bad as he does. So I may just fall for this and whatever else that he has up his sleeve that's intended for us to wake up next to each other in the morning, so I just listen to him.

Because it's been hard not being able to just wake up and climb on top of his rock-hard dick when he first wakes up in the mornings.

Sometimes I would even catch him before he even gets up to go and pee. So with that thought alone he's not going to have to work as hard as he may think he has to, because I'm ready for all of his bullshit tonight.

"Why didn't I get a call from one of you yesterday?" He asks with a confused-looking expression on his face.

"Because by the time we got home and settled in, it was kind of late, so we just called it a night and went to bed."

"Come on now, baby, you were too tired to call ya man?" He continues while looking at me and eagerly seeking a different answer.

"Lamar, you know that we have to make the decision on if we're going to be just friends or if we're going to continue to go toward something more. I just don't want to confuse the girls about what we are to each other right now, so let's just figure this out first. Then we can move forward in us staying connected every day like we used to."

"I've already made my decision!" He reminds me while appearing to be even more serious about his decision.

"We're already friends, and I've already told you that I want more. So I'll stop whatever you want me to stop if that's what it's going to take for us to be together."

"I don't want you to stop what you're doing because it's what I want you to do, I want you to stop and look at the situation for yourself. Then make your own decision on what you think is the smartest thing for you to do, don't do it for me. That's only going to end up hurting our relationship later anyway, especially if it's genuinely not what you really want to do."

"I understand what you're saying, CJ, I really do. But can we please talk about this later?"

25

"We've already done enough talking about it—it's time to see some actions, but you're right. We should leave it alone and enjoy a night free from arguments about it."

We both now agree to let it go, and just continue on with the night.

His brother Ken walks over to us and says. "Man, is everybody trying to be boo'd up tonight or what? Y'all need to save that shit for the bedroom and let's pop open some more bottles!"

We both laugh at Ken because he has so many kids that he can never really get free from to go out and have any real adult fun, unless Lamar or one of their friends just pops up at his house and makes him come along.

But Ken complains until he has everybody up laughing, eating, and clowning around for about two hours.

"Lamar, I only need like one more glass of wine and then I'm done for tonight. I'm just going to sit back and watch my girls do their thing."

"I got you, baby."

He assures me. "You can go ahead and get your drink on because none one of y'all will be driving tonight if it's left up to me."

He now places two glasses in front of me and fills them both to the very top with wine until they are almost overflowing.

"I have to meet Adrian in the morning, and this time I have to show up since I've stood her up twice before. So let's just move one of these glasses away from me because I don't want to be all sick and hung over in the morning." I inform him while passing one of the overly filled glasses down the table.

Seeing how Adrian has called and told me that some chick called her and told her that she's pregnant by Paul, and she believes her. So I know that she definitely needs a friend right now, and I'm going to make sure that I'm there for her no matter what.

26

Because I don't blame her for believing some other woman's word over Paul's word this time.

He's not going to be able to escape the scrutiny of how he's gotten some other woman pregnant within their marriage by lying and cheating on her all the time.

"Okay, CJ, if you're done then you're done."

Lamar grabs the bottle of wine and puts it back into the ice bucket and says.

"But I'm going to keep this bottle on ice just in case you change your mind."

"I won't need it but okay."

I now take a sip from my overly filled glass and continue to laugh at how much wine he's poured into my last glass.

CHAPTER 5
"CONTROLLING LOVE"

Adrian is one of the smartest women I know, although she's put up with a lot within her marriage. I think that now that she's been helping her mom take care of her dad for the past year or so, the stress of the doctors telling them that he may not survive another month is weighing heavy on her right now.

So for Paul to continue his bull crap is really sending a bold message of disrespect, because he knows how much she loves her dad. But I think the karma machine is gearing up to hit him in his face really hard one day.

Because she really has tried to do everything right to make their marriage work, regardless of how everyone is always telling her to just accept who he is and walk away.

Adrian and I went to school together, but then after graduation she landed a great job as a buyer for a popular clothing store chain.

She said that she was going to get as much information as she could in the fashion industry, because one day she would love to create and sell her own designs.

All she ever talked about was one day owning her own boutique, just like I always talked about owning my own magazine one day called *New Age News*, which I now own.

And it's one of the best-selling local magazines online and offline, because we have a great internet presence known for being very informative. Yet messy at times, so we keep the city talking about the latest news, as well as gossip.

And Adrian is welcomed to join us because it will help her to financially get back on her feet, so that she won't have to depend on Paul so much.

When they first met, it was at one of the stores that she was working for, and there was a murder in front of the store. And she and Paul were among the witnesses of the crime, so they had to stay and tell the police what they saw.

She told me how they had kept them there for so long that they had to bring them something to eat while they waited, and how she and Paul had started a conversation that they both found very interesting, and it later led to them flirting with each other until it was finally time to go.

He had no job, no vehicle, and no place to stay other than with his friends and family. So all he really had to offer was just a head full of ideas. And that made her iffy about being anything other than just friends with him, to avoid having another hard budgeting relationship like she's had in the past.

She said that she wanted someone who was just as financially stable as she was, or better.

But Paul was a struggling music producer who didn't get paid if no one bought his music.

But that day when they were waiting to be interviewed by the detectives, he somehow still managed to get her number with his impressive conversations about his music ideas and business plans. Because she eventually started bringing him around us all the time like he was her boyfriend, and she was proud of it.

We even used to tease her about how he must either just have a slick way with words, or he was just plain ole giving it to her good in the bedroom. Because he moved in with her only after about three months of dating.

Everybody, including her immediate family members knew how much she had fallen for him when she let him move in with her, because she never moves that fast with any man.

She told me that when she'd met some of his family members, his aunt told her that Paul was really book smart.

And then she showed her some of his honor plaques; along with several other certificates, awards, and other achievements that he'd made over the years that he'd never mentioned to her.

But when she asked him why wasn't he working in the dentistry field—since every certificate or achievement that he had was in that field.

He told her that he had a hard time adjusting back to things like that after losing his grandmother in a car accident. And that he had only been doing all of that to make her proud to see that she didn't fail in raising him. But he said that he's always wanted to be a dentist, and a music producer. So when a good-paying opportunity presented itself that allowed him to focus more on being a producer.

He took it, and while it got hard after his first paying contract was over, he still managed to survive financially as a music producer.

But fast forwarding to after they'd been together for a while, she asked him if he would ever consider going back to dental school at some point in his life. If she helped him to search for any available scholarships or grant money that he could potentially qualify for, due to his history of receiving so many honors in school before he quit. And his answer ended up being yes about a year after the question was asked, because they pulled together to get him everything he needed to get him back in school again as far as fees and past due balances and whatever else that he needed.

I even went with her to the mall to buy him new clothes and shoes to prepare him even more to go back to school fresh and dressed appropriately. And throughout all of that, they had broken up and gotten back together more times than I want to count.

I guess he tried to stay committed to her, but his many secrets just kept coming forward and showing her what kind of person he really is.

Although at one point Paul actually did step up and took over as head breadwinner for them, because he'd already had a clinical job set up and waiting for him after graduation.

She was then able to do exactly what she said that she always wanted to do if she ever had kids. She got to stay at home and take care of their children herself, instead of having to drop them off at a day care center while she would be at work.

She used to say that becoming a housewife was good for her because she loved taking care of Paul and their kids. And when the twins are old enough to speak up for themselves, then she would put her focus back onto having a successful career in the fashion industry.

But lately, she's been so unhappy that now she says that being a housewife isn't as fun as it used to be, and I'm sure that her change of heart is sprouting from several reasons.

Maybe it's because Paul is still abusing and neglecting her as a housewife, and she's really tired of it. Or maybe she's just now realizing that she's completely lost interest in anything outside of him and the twins. And it's prohibiting her original goals of being in fashion or anything else at this point.

And she told me that the weird part about her catching Paul was that the women were really in love with him and his lies.

And regardless of whether he had a job or not, they were still doing things for him, and he knew that he could get them to do whatever he wanted them to do at times. — While he hung around in the studios producing music.

But now days, since she has to force him to do what he should be doing as a father more than she should have to. She wants to leave him and just put him on child support now that he has partnered with two other dentists and opened an orthodontic clinic.

And I know that he's really messed up this time because this chick who's saying that she's pregnant by him gave her way more information about Paul than she should have been able to give.

So now that I'm pulling up to the restaurant to have breakfast with her, I can only hope that she's really ready to step away from him until she can truly decide what's best for her and the twins this time. Even if she ends up deciding to stay with him, she can at least say that she honestly took some time to evaluate things a little more this time before she makes her decision.

And surprisingly, she looks more relieved than sad, as I watch her walk across the parking lot towards me after I pull into a parking space.

"You look beautiful, Adrian!" I yell with a big smile on my face as I get out of my car.

"Thank you, Chase! You said that you didn't want to see me in any more sweatpants, so I decided to surprise you by dressing up today!"

"Well, it's a wonderful surprise because you look great! I was just thinking about how much I miss your style of fashion, and how I just knew that you would be wearing a T-shirt and sweatpants today!"

"Nah," she now brings me up to date. "That's why I'm here. I'm ready to take my life back, but first I have to get out of this marriage. And I'm going to need your help so come on and let's go inside and sit down."

"Okay, come on, because I'm ready to help you in any way I can. Girl, you and I both know that you deserve to be happier than you've been lately."

So now after walking inside and waiting to be seated, a waiter soon comes to seat us and gives us menus while asking us if we would like some coffee.

We politely decline the coffee and request to have some orange juice and water.

"CJ, I can't believe that I stayed with this man after he's given me two sexually transmitted diseases within this marriage." Adrian professes as soon as the waiter leaves the table.

"I feel like the dumbest chick in the world right now, and to be honest, a part of me actually feels like I deserve everything that I'm going through. Because I should have known better than to take him back after he cheated on me the first time."

"First of all, you didn't deserve any of that, so you have to stop blaming yourself for forgiving him for what he did to you. You did everything that you could do to try to make your marriage work, including stay with him after he'd given you the STDs. But girl, sometimes we just fight so hard to hold on to something that even God himself is trying to pull apart for our own good."

"You're right about that because all I cared about was the fact that I always had both of my parents living under the same roof with me when I was growing up. And I wanted my kids to grow up with both parents being in the same household with them, so I didn't care what I had to deal with to keep us together. Even when it seemed like God really was trying to show me signs of Paul's bad behavior. I ignored them by blaming Satan and everybody else but Paul, because I wanted us to be together as a family so badly."

"Well, like I said, you've done everything that you could do to try to make it work. But at the end of the day, it's going to take more than just you working on the relationship for it to work. But right now, one of the most important things is that you move forward knowing that you can still raise the twins up right even if both parents aren't living under the same roof with them."

"I believe that, and CJ, I'm going to do everything I can to make sure that they are good because I'm over trying to save Paul. Because another reason why I stayed with him was because he has been through so much in his life, and sometimes he would be a lot more than just convincing when he would say that he was going to kill himself if I ever left him. He's done things that would play back in my head that makes me think that he'll probably go ahead and finally just pull the trigger once and for all if I actually left him and never came back."

"What do you mean finally pull the trigger once and for all?"

"I mean, I've seen him do things like take his gun and put it to his head and threaten to pull the trigger when I actually got up to pack our bags to leave him. He would kiss the twins and tell them good-bye, and that he loves them and then tell me that he don't have nothing else to live for if he ever loses us, so he would rather die than to live without us. But the reality is that if he really cared all that much about losing us, then he wouldn't be out here cheating on me all the time."

"Exactly."

I agree and express my opinion.

"And for him to be putting that gun to his head in front of you is so fucked up when he's the one out here cheating and messing up."

34

"That's what I told him, but his threats don't bother me anymore because now I can see that he only does things like that to try to scare me into staying with him."

"That's true, I think it's a scare tactic too. But knowing of what he's done in the past, you know that Paul is not going to just give you guys up without a fight. Now are you really ready to battle with him? Because things may get uglier than they've ever gotten before after he realizes that it's truly over between y'all?"

"I believe that he's going to try to make my life a living hell after I leave him and really file for this divorce for real. But yes, I'm ready for it. I know that even if I share custody of the twins with him, he's still going to make me wish that I'd never met him so it's whatever."

"Outside of being blessed with the twins, sometimes you already wish that you had never met him anyway, so you'll be fine. And he'll probably let his unwillingness to let go screw him in the end anyway. But now that you're ready to move on, let's just get ready to do whatever you think we need to do to get you where you need to be. And I'm so excited and happy for you because I can tell that you're finally tired of that shit, and you're ready to live happier."

I now quickly pick up the menu to place my order as the waitress comes back and asks us if we know what we want. — We both place our orders then develop a plan A and a plan B on how we're going to pack their things, their furniture and everything. And just leave him this time instead of her putting him out.

She really seems to be ready to put one foot in front of the other and let her will to leave him guide her into happiness. And I'm going to be right here with her every step of the way, because she's going to need a true friend in her corner to lean on during this time especially.

CHAPTER 6
"PREPARING TO PARTY"

C hris's barbershop, Studio Cutz, always has this big summer jam event that seems to bring half the city out to party with them.

And Chris has a lot of different pictures of politicians and celebrities of whom he's had the pleasure of servicing, posted on the walls of the barbershop. And he'll usually just get with a few radio personalities and local celebrities who don't mind helping him to promote the party.

But we still all come together to help him make the party a big success every year, although nowadays, he really doesn't need any of our help because people look forward to attending whether we promote it or not.

But his girlfriend, Kris, and I still do a lot of promoting for him now that we can get along long enough to be in the same room together without wanting to rip each other's head off.

Chris introduced me and Kris to each other when they first started getting serious a few years ago, but we couldn't get along for nothing in this world because I didn't like some of the wild and crazy things that she did in regards to him.

And I let it be known to her and everyone else around us how much I didn't like it, that's why at one point I would've never referred to her as my friend under any circumstances.
But thanks to Chris, we've now worked through our issues and have been more like friends than enemies lately.
Chris had gotten with the both of us and told us that we might as well work out our problems because we were going to have to be around each other at some point or another anyway.
So we ended up doing just that and have been working things out ever since, especially after I witnessed him take it upon himself to explain to her in front of me that he and I are going to be friends regardless of what's going on in his life.
I knew right then that I no longer needed to let anything that she say bother me because that was enough proof of how much he valued our friendship.
She also eventually saw that I would never disrespect him or her by trying to interfere with their relationship in any way at all, although she still used to get on my nerves with that smart-ass mouth of hers. — And I wanted to say things that I knew would hurt her feelings so badly, but I just kept my mouth shut to keep the peace no matter how mad she made me.
I never threw it in her face that Chris and I actually had a crush on each other that one time went a lot further than just a crush a few months before they met. But as his friend, I knew not to say anything due to the fact that he would've told her for himself if he wanted her to know.
And we've already managed to keep our one night of passionate sex a secret that only he and I know about for this long, so I surely didn't, and still don't see any reasons for me to release that information because of her smart mouth when we pretty much have everything under control.
We also care too much for our friendship to ruin it for a romantic relationship that we both know won't survive.

Although at one point people did used to say that Chris and I were always flirting by how we would laugh at absolutely everything that came out of each other's mouths, but regardless of all that. We still would never hurt Lamar and Kris by telling them what happened when it truly was a onetime-only thing.

But nowadays, everybody can see that it's totally innocent, and he's truly just a friend who has my back like I have his. Because our loyalty always outweigh everything and everybody even now, just without as many women trying to come between our friendship.

Because before Kris came into his life, Chris had so many women claiming him that it was just plain ole ridiculous. And they were always arguing or fighting over him or about him like he was a bag of money or something. He had hood chicks, professional chicks, white chicks, black chicks, Latino chicks, and more.

He says that I always over exaggerate when I talk about him and his many female friends, because according to him, he didn't really have as many woman as people thought he did. Although I still believe that he had more than he's willing to admit.

However, these days he seems to be a changed man judging by how well he's revamped his ways, because sometimes he calls me just to tell me how he's feeling about things. And lately he's mostly been talking about his son and how much he loves old cars, and every now and then he'll mention a few things about his brothers because there are so many of them.

But for now, it's all about the summer jam party. So I'm headed to his barbershop to pick up Kris so that she can go with me to buy some shoes to wear to the party. — I tried, but I couldn't buy what I want to wear to this party at any of the boutiques that I visited. Because what I want has to be something very exclusive and with a lot of sex appeal.

And while I saw a lot of good options, I still couldn't find anything that I really wanted. But fortunately, I'm lucky enough to have found exactly what I want to wear online, but my shoes have become a challenge.

Kris and I have decided to do some shopping together because she's actually in need of a dress, shoes, and a bag.

And as I pull up to the shop, the lot is packed with cars as usual, so I park in the handicapped space up front that no one ever parks in even if he or she is handicapped.

Studio Cutz is one of the largest barbershops in our city, equipped with ten to twelve giant booths with complimentary flat-screen TVs posted throughout the building for people to watch while they wait to be serviced.

And every section is filled with someone cutting hair, braiding, twisting dreadlocks, or something.

And I really admire how well he has it all organized because it's not your average-looking barbershop with goodies in the back. Someone does sell hair, candles, oils, and a few other novelties in the shop, but it's legit and set up very professionally and neat like you would see in the shopping malls.

But he still has a different kind of vibe going on with its design that makes you just want to hang out with them all day.

It's like a Bob Marley type of scenery with yet a hip-hop/poetic type of vibe going on that's really interesting.

Chris himself, I must say is quite the unpredictable type outside of being hilarious. He stands well over six feet tall and has really nice-looking dreadlocks, and he has some bling on the bottom row of his teeth.

And the bling doesn't cover his entire bottom row of teeth, he only has one on the far-left bottom tooth and one on the far-right bottom tooth. Just those two and that's it, ultimately he has a gorgeous smile like he could have been some sort of toothpaste model if he wanted to be.

Even with those diamonds in his mouth I think that he can still be in a great teeth commercial, it's just that those diamonds seem to bring out his sexy thuggish swagger. But still with a hint that he can handle his business professionally because his complete smile is awesome.

And he really is a professional because Chris is very stern and serious when it comes to his businesses, and I know that's how he's become so successful.

He owns an apartment building that has ten expensive units that are all rented out to residents, and they have a privacy gate to keep the loiterers out, and to protect the landscaping and residents.

He also owns a store inside of the West County Mall called Legs & Feet, where they only sell jeans and shoes.

He also owns a Locksmithing company specializing in extreme locks, keys, safes, door closers, and other locksmithing needs.

We had sex because I was so turned on by how together he was with his businesses not only in how he thinks, but also in what he does.

It's like he's so street-smart and also book smart, and it shows, and with him being so fun to be around. My panties dropped, and so did my belief that a man can't just talk a woman completely out of her underwear without it ever being her intention to do so in the first place.

Because after a long night of drinking expensive French vodka, and discussing how close we are as friends, it seemed like us having sex was the one and only thing that was left for us to do. But anyway, as of now while at the shop waiting for Kris, I walk over to mess with Poolo because he's always offering to rub my feet every time I come into the shop. Even if I stop by and he's not working, I'll have someone to call him so that I can mess with him about how much I actually need my feet rubbed every time he's not at work.

"CJ, you need to go ahead and let me sop you up with a biscuit!"
Poolo says while chuckling when he sees me walking over to his booth.
"Whatever, Poolo! You always want to touch my feet, now you want to sop me up! What's next?"
And before he can respond to me, Kris comes from the back looking very zaftig dressed in my favorite color. And with a new hairdo and perfectly done makeup looking almost as if she has none on at all.
She's wearing a purple fitted bodysuit that's not too tight or too loose, and looking very classy because not everyone can step into a full bodysuit and wear it like she's wearing it.
On top of it fitting her body perfectly where it needs to fit, it has pockets and a few specks of silver at the top that matches her sandals and her bag. — And her jewelry is shining just as bright as her lip gloss, and as bright as the smile that she's wearing while walking towards me.
"I see that you're looking quite fabulous today, Kris! Chris better watch out because all eyes will be on you everywhere we go looking like this!"
"Oh, so what are you saying?"
She shouts at me jokingly with her hands on her hips.
"Are you saying that I'm not always fabulous or what?"
"Nah, honey, as a matter of fact. Like myself, you're always fabulous. I'm just saying that today that outfit is like whoa, look at me now Bitches!"
And after I continue to talk about her and how she looks, she laughs and turns around modeling a smile and telling me that she's trying to get Chris to take her on a cruise trip if she can ever get him to stop acting so distant towards her.
"My travel agency friend is coming to the party, and she has some kind of specialty getaway cruise that she was telling me

about that would really be good for us." She says. "And I want to set something up for me and Chris to try to reconnect, since he's been acting so closed in and quiet. So I was hoping to show him a curve or two today, thinking that maybe he would change his mind about going. But so far the bodysuit isn't working because he's still saying that he don't want to go, but don't worry about it because I'll get his attention in one way or another." We both now leave Poolo's booth to walk over to Chris's work area.

"Well, girl, if you keep looking like this then I think that you're going to get that cruise trip plus a few other things along with it!"

We both giggle like teenagers as if Chris, whom we are now standing in front of, can't hear us.

We know that he can hear us but we don't care because I now want them to take the trip as well, because they really haven't been anywhere by themselves since she had little Chris.

And I think that it would be good for them to get out and away from everybody. But I am wondering what's up with him acting so distant towards her, when everything seemed to be cool with them according to our conversation the last time he and I talked about their relationship.

And he can't just start acting like that with her after everything that we've been through to get me and her to this point of finally having a conversation without attitudes and getting smart with each other. — We hated each other, but now as her friend, I genuinely want to help her. And I think Chris would've told me if he wasn't feeling her anymore, so maybe she's done something that he just haven't told me about yet.

But while hearing everything that Kris and I are saying about how good a cruise trip would be for them, Chris hasn't said a word. He's just listening in silence while shaking his head from left to right at everything that we're saying, like he really isn't

42

interested in going on any kind of cruise trip with her anytime soon.

"Don't worry about it, CJ, let's just change the subject. Then he'll speak because as long as we're talking about us, he won't have shit to say until he feels like it." Kris clamors as she turns that big smile of hers upside down.

"Girl, it's OK, y'all will be good sooner or later. He's probably just mad because we're about to go and shop until we drop on his debit card!"

And I don't help much in breaking his silence because all he says is, "huh."

"I'm sure that y'all will deal with this later Kris, but you're going to get that cruise."

"Huh," he says again. While I now give up after he remains quiet when usually he would be saying something funny or cocky like. 'Good thing we didn't ask you for your help at all on the subject, now all we need is for you to be quiet.'

But after he continues to give us a lot of unusual behavior, we soon proceed to leave because Kris eventually turns around and takes off walking toward the door without saying anything else.

And when we get in the car, she says. "I'm not sure how much more of this I can take with him acting like this—for real. You know that he didn't say anything back to you because of me, and did you see how he was looking at me?"

"Yep, and I've never really seen him just shut down on nobody like that, so what's going on with y'all? I mean at first I thought that it couldn't be that bad or you wouldn't have had such a big smile on your face when you came from the back of the shop. But now I don't know, because I can see that you're hurting, and I can tell that something isn't right for real by how he's acting. Maybe it's just that he's got a lot going on right now, so just try sitting down and talking to him one-on-one without bringing up the cruise again."

"Every time I try to sit down and have a conversation with him, he shuts down and starts acting all rude and disrespectful and shit," she says while sadly looking away. "I'm just tired of it."

"Rude and disrespectful, that don't sound like Chris to me. What's really going on with y'all, Kris? And be honest because this isn't how y'all usually be, especially in public."

"I was hoping that you could tell me what's really going on with us because he sure as hell don't tell me anything about him or what he's thinking anymore. I used to worry about different women trying to creep back into his life, but CJ that's over. I'm sure that he's not communicating with any of them. He's too busy, and he wouldn't give those bitches the time of day anymore, even if he could fit them into his schedule. I just can't figure out what the problem is because he has completely shut me out." Lowering her head and dropping a tear into her lap, she begins to cry.

"Well, if you've already tried talking to him and he's not listening, let's just figure something else out because he hasn't said anything to me about you guys having any problems."

"It's just crazy to me because lately I haven't done anything to Chris for him to treat me like this."

She continues to cry and gaze out of the window.

"I don't know what's happening between us right now, but he's not about to just keep shutting me out like this."

"Don't cry, Kris. But I understand what you're saying. And I'm going to try to help you as much as I can if you want me to, we'll just have to get on top of seeing what's really bothering him and fix it."

I now give her a Kleenex from my armrest to dry her eyes with before I drive away. "Everything's going to be okay, you'll see."

Kris is crazy with a capital C, so it's unlike her to wear her heart on her sleeve like this in front of anybody—especially in front of me—so things must be extremely bad with them.

44

I only get to hear about how she used to cut and stab chicks and spray them with bleach and alcohol when she got mad, and there's never really any crying being done by her.

And not to paint a bad picture of her as a person, but that's just usually what our one-on-one conversations are about sometimes.

So I'm actually shocked and surprised to see her showing me this complete change of emotions about how she's feeling.

It's a big jump from her explaining how she would call child services on the women that Chris would mess around with who had kids.

She would report crazy allegations of abuse without even knowing anything about the woman or her children.

But I'm still sympathetic to her because I know that she's truly hurting right now, and I'm going to help her as much as I can without overstepping my bounds as a loyal friend to Chris.

I'm just compelled by my thoughts of remembering how she had put zip lock bags of sugar and some chocolate bars in the tail pipe of some other woman's car whom she had found out about. But she didn't even know if he was really cheating on her with that woman or not, but she still went and flattened the woman's tires and burst the headlights and two back windows out of her car. And as if all of that wasn't enough, she had printed a picture of the woman and her child from the internet and left it on her windshield.

It was like she planned things like that out and completed her task every time, she's even purposely placed razor blades inside of her hair and then went out and started a fight over Chris.

She would do horrible things to make the women suffer for talking to him. But I told her a long time ago that she was way too pretty for that stupid ghetto bullshit, but at that time she only heard what she wanted to hear.

She said that she just couldn't help it when she would flip out like that, but I knew that she could help it because of how she acted after Chris explained to her that I would be in his life whether she liked it or not. And there are plenty of times that I can recall when she was killing mad at me before and after he told her that, and we never had any of those type of problems.

So that let me know that she could indeed control her behavior if she really wanted to, I just believe that she knew who she could mess with and who she couldn't mess with in that manner.

That's why we've just been working things out and continuing to try to be friends because she knows not to come at me like that. But now as I drive us to our first shopping spot, she says. "I know that I can get a little special sometimes, but ever since that time Chris hit me. I haven't said or did anything else crazy because I thought that I was going to have to go to the emergency room after still having a headache for about two days after that happened."

She continues while looking out of the window.

"But then I figured that I deserved to be in pain because he only did it because I had threatened to cut him with a knife one night when he had come home super late after not answering his phone all night. He's never hit me before, but that night he was going to have to either hit me, kill me, or explain to me why he wasn't answering his phone because I was mad as hell. And it got bad in our house that night for real because we were physically fighting hard, and that's never happened before. But all I could think about was all of the different women who were calling him, mixed with him coming in so late. So I waited for him to fall asleep, and then I went into our bedroom and woke him up with a knife in my hand and demanded an explanation."

Now looking at me instead of the window, she says. "But CJ, I knew that I wasn't going to cut or stab him or anything like that, but I guess he thought differently so we fought until I broke away and locked myself in the basement. And he kept trying to get me to come back upstairs, but I was too scared to open the door, especially after everything that I had already put him through even before that night. All he kept asking me was why did I have the knife if I wasn't planning on using it, and it sounded like he was going to burst through the door and beat the hell out of me for everything that I'd done. And with his skills I knew that if he really wanted to come through that door, he could have. And when he didn't, I just sat there and cried and cried, especially when he started saying how he's been nothing but good to me and treated me with respect. I cried so hard because he really had been good to me and treated me with respect, and maybe I shouldn't have done what I did since he's never not answered his phone for me before. But I felt like just because he didn't do things in my face, that didn't mean that he was innocent. Even though I had heard him telling females to stop calling him, but they would still call him anyway. And I know that may seem to be out of his control, but CJ you know Chris could've really stopped whatever he wanted to stop, but didn't. He would hang up on them and think that's all that needed to be done, instead of really stopping them. That's why I went crazy on him because he could've did more to stop them, but I was just mad about everything. But I'll always regret the night I went in there with that knife for the rest of my life, because things just haven't been the same between us since then. I mean when y'all would see us happy, we really were happy, but now we're nowhere near as happy as we used to be. Because no matter how many times I tell him that I honestly was not about to do anything to him, I feel like he just doesn't believe me. Nor did he ever really forgive me for doing that, even though he says that all of that is in the past, and he's not tripping off of it anymore. I don't think he really forgave me."

"Well, Kris, it's like you said. Chris can stop whatever he wants to stop, and he's still with you so that's a plus. And I see that things aren't perfect, but you know that y'all wouldn't still be together at all if he really didn't want to be there. And of course he's going to be acting distant if you pulled a knife on him, but then again you said that was in the past so it's probably something else that's bothering him. I didn't know that you had pulled a knife on him, but you guys have grown a lot since he had all of those women and stuff. Although I must say that I am surprised that y'all stayed together after that, or that you're even still alive after you did that."

"I'm surprised, too," she sobs.

"But that really was a long time ago, and we've supposedly moved on from it, but things just haven't been the same since that night. He just be acting really shitty toward me sometimes, and nowadays whenever we do talk, it's only about little Chris. So I'm feeling like he should have just stopped fucking with me altogether if he only stayed with me just to treat me like shit."

"I understand. But Kris, I just don't think that he would have stayed with you after that if he didn't love you and want to be with you. But he really is acting shitty so I feel where you're coming from, even if the both of you have already agreed to put the whole knife thing behind you. It's hard to move forward if he really hasn't put it behind him for real, but you have to admit that it's not easy to forgive somebody that you love after they have woke you up with a knife in their hands demanding anything. But I'll let you know if I find out anything that can help you because I really thought that you two were cool until today."

"Nah, we're far from cool, and I appreciate you helping me because I honestly don't know what else to do at this point. Like I said, I wish I could take back everything that happened that night and even before then. But I can't. And that night may not even have anything to do with how he's been feeling lately, I just want to know if that's what's really bothering him, or if it's something else. Because I don't know how much more I can take of him acting like this towards me." She now shakes her head and reaches into the armrest for another Kleenex.

"Just dry your eyes and let's do some shopping to try to clear your head for a little while. Then after we're done, we can try to figure something out that will maybe help you end up getting that cruise trip after all."

"Girl, I know that he's not going on that cruise, but maybe we can get him to at least start back talking to me about what's wrong with him."

CHAPTER 7
"CABIN READY"

The sun is shining as bright as it ever has on this beautiful Saturday morning, and my girls and I have appointments to get our nails done.

But I think I may let them join me in getting facials and pedicures today as well, since I'm in such a good mood after finding everything that I needed yesterday at the stores with Kris. I think I'll splurge a little today.

Besides, I'm not sure who enjoys our pampered days out more—me or my daughters. We always have so much fun when we hang out.

And later today, after we spend this family time together during the morning, they have plans to go over to their aunt's house for a 'movie sequels slumber party'.

And parties like that tend to help us feel better about life and the people around us. And both of my girls are very excited about getting with their friends and cousins, just as much as I am about this summer jam party, and this upcoming five-day getaway at the cabin with my friends.

Last year, I was unable to attend this yearly cabin trip where Chris offers to rent out rooms to people as a luxury getaway for after his summer jam party.

The cabin is owned by two wealthy Jewish brothers who owes Chris a big favor, and the only thing that he wanted from them was to be able to rent out their cabin at a discounted rate whenever he wants it.

So they have it all worked out for when their family isn't using it, or if they're not renting it out for seminars, retreats, or just general company business. Chris can get it, and they always make sure that he gets it whenever he asks for it. But his party is always around the same time every year, and this year is no different.

But there's only a limited amount of people who can get a room at the cabin, so he usually only invites his closest friends.

The first time that I visited I was blown away by how much we could do out there because it's definitely not your average cabin in the woods.

And Chris said that since he rents it out so much, they're letting him get it for free this year, so no one has to pay to go this time.

So, as Studio Cutz had the city wired up after inviting everybody who's anybody out to party with them, it was great.

Although if you haven't made a name for yourself, or if you don't know somebody who can get you through the doors when you arrive. Then you have to stand outside and wait in line, or pay a ridiculous entry fee to get in.

And it seemed like the more people left the party, the more people was coming inside because once you walked out, you couldn't get back in without paying again.

So we all showed up and had fun all night because security brought their A game, and they handled any signs of confusion because there was no violence at all throughout the entire night.

And then after the party was a success, those of us who had to get up early, we took what few hours we had left to go and get some rest and to prepare to get together for our cabin getaway.

CHAPTER 8
"LET'S HAVE FUN"

It's nine o'clock in the morning, and we've all come together and tightly packed three vehicles with as much stuff as we can before taking this four-hour drive to the cabin.

And when we finally arrive at the cabin, it's just as beautiful as I remembered it to be the last time I was out here.

Upon going inside, we all pick a room before we separate to go and unpack. And since Lamar would never let me come out here without him whether we're together or not, he's with me.

And we choose the room next to Sky and Chad, while Chris and Kris take the first room next to us.

And Rayci and Markus are on the other side of the hallway with two of Chris's friends and their girlfriends.

Everyone is coupled and preparing to have a good time while unpacking and getting comfortable for the next five days.

And everything is usually planned out for the first two days of us being here, while the other three days are free for all to do whatever they want to do.

But as for now, the music is already playing when I come from our room after unpacking my bags.

Rayci is the first person to start making drinks.

She told us that she has this new slushy drink recipe that will get us hot and cool us off all at the same time.

But the men are saying that they don't want any slushy drinks because they have their own variety of white and dark liquors.

Ultimately, we're all just glad to be away from everybody and everything, and we're looking forward to relaxing in this beautiful place.

And since we're now all together, we decide to figure out what we will be eating for dinner our first night here.

The cabin owners' company security house isn't too far away, and they have employees who oversee everything concerning the cabin, as well as the giant golf course that's on the other side of the trees and beautiful scenery.

And although we know that the meals that they deliver are already included in our stay, we still like to cook and prepare our own meals whenever we feel like it. And they only serve lunch and dinner anyway, so we brought a lot of our own groceries.

But Markus and Chad goes and get some cards, dominoes, and a cooler filled with alcohol after we all decide on the foods that we want to order.

While Sky and Kris says that they are about to put on their bathing suits and take a dip in the pool because of how inviting the water looks. And just about everyone else here, including me. Feels the exact same way about the water, and we're probably about to get in it with them.

But first, I have to see if Lamar still wants to talk to me about what's really going on between us. So I walk over to him and give him a cup of ice, and tell him that if he still wants to talk. Then coming into the pool behind me would be a wise choice for him right about now. Although honestly, all I really want to do is show off my hot-pink and brown float that I bought just to match my hot-pink and brown bathing suit.

He and I have five days to decide finally once and for all what we're going to do as far as us officially breaking up, or getting back together.

So I'm not really concerned with that right now, and I kind of don't even want to talk about it for real, but we'll see.

Lamar ends up following me into our room to put on his swim trunks.

"Okay, Lamar, so now that you've put on your trunks and everything. Here, take this float and pump to blow it up with because you have to get out so that I can change. Just take all of that with you because I don't want you to see me in my swimsuit until I can see how I look in it first." I gesture while handing him my float and a pump for him to take with him.

Although I'm lying—because I already know how I look in my swimsuit—I just want him to see me in it at the same time as everyone else.

"I don't know why you want me to get out while you change, it's not like I haven't seen every inch of your body already. As a matter of fact, I probably know your body better than you do."

Looking me up and down, and now looking around the room he says. "And how much skin will you be showing anyway? Because I may need to inspect you before you come out of here."

He now throws a towel over his shoulder and sits down on the bed like he isn't about to leave just yet.

"Inspect me? Um, I'm single and free to do whatever I want to do, remember? So if I want to come out of here damn near naked, I have the right to do so as a single adult. Even though I have more respect for myself, you, and my friends and their men to not come out of here naked. But I will let you know that

I'm about to wear the hell out of this swimsuit though, and hopefully it's not too revealing in your opinion."

"See, I guess I am going to leave the room on that note since you always have to throw bullshit comments into our mix about how single you are and shit! When obviously we're out here together, so you're really not all that motherfucking single, while you're pointing shit out!"

He squawks while getting up to walk out and somewhat slamming the door as he exit the room.

But what he doesn't know is that my heart is kind of telling me that as soon as we get in the pool, and can get a private conversation going. I'm thinking about telling him that I'm ready to get back with him if we can just come up with a solution to our main problem once and for all.

It's almost like we never broke up anyway, I just don't want us to be thinking about something as big as marriage before taking things slow again as boyfriend and girlfriend. Because in my opinion, neither one of us is ready for marriage, and if we can agree to disagree on that.

While we work on figuring it all out together, then maybe we can move forward with making things even better within our relationship to go even farther one day.

But as for now, I've just finished changing into my swimsuit, so I have to double-check myself in the mirror before leaving the room to get into the pool. Because I know that a few heads are going to turn as soon as they see me coming down the hallway.

And thankfully the main head has the biggest smile on his face when I come out, I guess he's had a little time to cool down from going off on me. Because Lamar's frown from earlier has turned into a smile because he doesn't look mad at all.

"Damn, baby, you look like a pink piece of candy!" He says while walking towards me. "Um, and you smell like a piece, too," he hugs me tightly while sniffing on my neck.

"I thought you were mad at me?"

"I am mad at you," he continues to look me over.

"But you still look good as a mothafucka! And I didn't come all the way out here to beef with you, we can do that shit back at the crib!"

We both now smile when he says. "You look and smell like some candy for real, baby."

"I bet I taste like a piece, too."

We laugh and now walk out back to get in the pool.

And when we get into the pool and start mingling with everyone, Lamar holds on to me as we float across the pool chitchatting. But Sky swiftly approaches us in the water, "Lamar, I have something important to tell my friend, and it's girl stuff so you can't listen."

"And what's that supposed to mean? I should leave so that y'all can talk about people?"

He says while shaking his head. "You might as well say whatever you have to say right now because I'm not going nowhere."

And he really doesn't move, so she does exactly what he says because she now grabs onto my float and whispers into my ear.

"The light-skinned chick who's here with one of Chris's friends is trying to get with Lamar."

I now pause for a second because out of all the things that could have waited to be said, this would top the list for the both of us. Especially when Sky is the main one who's always saying how if another woman can just take your man by flirting with him, then he probably wasn't yours anyway.

So for her to make it her business just to tell me this, I know that we must really need to talk, on top of the fact that I can see the frustration on her face even from how she came over here with such a serious demeanor that's usually not like her. — So now I tell Lamar that I really need to talk to her by myself for a minute, because it really is important. But he looks at me while throwing his hands in the air while laughing and yelling.

"So you're just going to play me out like that, Chase?"

"I'll make it up to you later if you'll just give me three or four minutes with her."

I bargain with him while he says that he's definitely going to hold me to making it up to him.

"CJ, if I didn't think that this bitch was up to no good, I would've waited and just said something to you later. But this is why I hate it when Chris invites new people out here with us!" She vents while I interrupt her.

"I knew from the look on your face and from how you came over here that something isn't right, so what's going on, and which chick is it again?"

"Well, when we first got here, the light-skinned chick with the short haircut made a few comments to her friend about Lamar. And you know that I'll hurt a bitch for being on some uncalled-for bullshit for no reason, but I just somewhat ignored what she was saying about him at first, because Lamar is fine and well-known and everything. But what made my temperature rise was when I came from my room and went into the kitchen. She and her friend was already in there, and she was telling her that you and Lamar had just gone into the bedroom. And although I couldn't hear them well enough to hear everything that she was saying, I heard enough to know that they're out here on some bullshit. Especially when her friend said that if she can get him, then she's a bad bitch for real. So I put a smile on my face and walked into the kitchen to join their conversation. I politely asked them what were they talking about because I'm a bad bitch, too. And instead of smiling with me, they both looked startled and nervous like I had just walked in on something. And when I asked them why did they get so quiet? They just stood there looking stupid and confused before they lied and said that they were just talking about how they felt like some bad bitches out here in this nice cabin. So I said awe, and then told them that after they were done in the kitchen, they should come and get into the pool with us. And then I went ahead and just left to come and get in the pool, but before I made it all the way out here. I turned around to go back inside to get a bottled water, because that's what I originally went into the kitchen for in the first place. But CJ, as soon as I made it back into the kitchen, the light-skinned one said that it would be wrong to go after somebody else's man. But Lamar don't have a ring on his finger, she said that she remembers him from dating some girl that she went to high school with. And her friend just kept cosigning everything that she was saying, and talking about how every man out here is fine as fuck. And if she would've known this shit, then they would have tried to come out here way before now. And when I tell you that it took everything in me to not mess up this trip for everybody after personally hearing this bitch say all of that—it literally took damn near everything in my being to stop me from saying something to them. But I'm telling you right now that there's nothing on this earth that's going to stop me from confronting these hoes about what I heard! I just told myself that the best thing for me to do is to take what they were saying and just hold it until after I talk to you. Because I know that we just got here, and everybody is having such a good time right now, so I wasn't about to let these simple bitches ruin our trip due to me walking in there and fucking both of them up. So I ended up keeping my cool because I know that I'll get my issues dealt with because there are no passes for this type of shit. I know that you're not going to let it pass either, but I'm just saying that I'm going to get at that friend of hers for you, since she's such a fucking cheerleader. She's all mine to break in half, and you can mark my words on that shit because it's a promise."

"Oh wow."
I respond. "So they were smiling and being all overly friendly with me earlier like they were trying to get to know me, but I really was too busy and couldn't talk to them at the time. So now my thing is that I never let my guard down to any woman when it comes to any man, but that sneaky disrespectful shit like trying to get him while I'm right here with him is just stupid. She obviously don't know that I don't play those type of games while they're trying to play with me, so I guess I'm just going to have to show them who I am. But I agree with you, I don't want to ruin things for us and everybody else out here over their thirsty asses. So I'll let you know how I want to handle them after we get out of this pool for sure, but you can trust and believe that after we're done with them. They'll never go after nobody else's man."
"Exactly, and I hope that you come up with something fast because my patience is wearing very thin already."
"I will, because this is apparently bothering you more than it's bothering me so I will definitely get on top of it when we get out. You know that I'm not tripping off of it too much because I'm used to women wanting Lamar, and being willing to do just about anything for his attention. But Lamar knows what he has, so I'm not worried, and I'm trying not to underestimate anything. But I'm sure that he'll pass on this one. But I do understand your frustration with how they came out here hunting for men and shit, and that's what's pissing me off, too. But just try to ignore them as much as you can because she and her friend are coming towards the pool right now, and I want to see them in action before I say anything."
"Okay, Chase, but this just may not turn out to be such a good trip after all. Because you know that you will end up hitting one of them just as quickly as I will, but okay, let's wait until we get out."

"Depending on how this light-skinned one is about to start acting will determine if I hit her or not, but I won't let her comments ruin this much-needed trip for us if I can help it. Now her actions on the other hand can shut this whole thing down, because I'm not going to tolerate being disrespected by anybody. But for now fuck her and her friend because Lamar is not even thinking about that girl, and like I said, she'll see me when I get out. I just want to reintroduce myself to them very ladylike before I say or do anything ratchet, but trust me. Sky, we're on the same page with this. And if you want to get at that friend of hers, you can, but first let's see how they are about to be acting out here."

"Okay, we can just issue out these ass whippings later."

She says as we both laugh at how much she just can't wait to get at them, but we both agree to leave it alone until later.

Lamar and I reconnect and float across the pool and find a spot so that we can chitchat and enjoy each other as much as possible, regardless of how everyone else is now in the pool with us and enjoying themselves as well.

I take this time to make his day happier by letting him know that I've officially made a decision regarding us.

"I want us to get back together, Lamar, but only as boyfriend and girlfriend."

"Boyfriend and girlfriend?"

"Yes, boyfriend and girlfriend because there are still too many issues between us to go any further than that right now. I just really need for you to understand that if we're already having a hard time committing, or even agreeing on something as important as your lifestyle. You have to see that taking our relationship further is a disaster waiting to happen if we just move forward and get married without fixing our issues first."

"I get it, at least I can say that I'm glad that you're taking me back, that's a start." He says while smiling.

"Because you've been killing me with all of that talking about you being single like I don't mean shit to you."

He now comes closer to me for a hug after I say that I'll never act like he doesn't mean shit to me.

Suddenly, Chris, Kris, and Rayci float in our direction, and Chris asks. "Lamar, what is Chase over here talking about? How we're about to beat them in this game right quick?"

"What game?"

I interfere. "Who said that we're about to play a game?"

"I did, Betty Boop, now cut out all of that hugging and come on over here so y'all can get ya asses beat!"

"It's funny how you're always talking so much trash when we're about to play a game, until you start losing."

I immediately jog his memory as my conversation with Lamar cease.

"Just get off of that float and come on and get served like everybody else."

He continues while coming towards me like he's about to do something that I'm not going to approve of. So I immediately put my sunglasses on top of my head and get off of my float, although I know that he won't flip me over or anything like that. But he will get on my nerves with his challenges and high-strung competitiveness so much that I may actually flip myself over, so that I won't have to listen to him. I've been friends with Chris longer than I've been friends with anyone out here, including Sky and Lamar, so I know exactly how he is.

He and I officially bonded and became close through a mutual friend, but I already kind of knew him ever since I was in elementary school through my cousin, whom he is still good friends with even now.

And it's not all fun and jokes all the time with us because we've had a few ups and downs within our friendship, but that's what has made us stay so close throughout the years.

61

But we've always had each other's back no matter what and that's for sure, and if there's one thing that I know in this life. It's that if I want or need any one man for anything on this earth—after seeking Christ first—I know that I can most definitely call on Chris for absolutely anything, and he will be there for me without a question.

But I would never let Lamar hear me say that because he would go berserk, although he knows that I would call on Chris if I were ever in need, because Chris is known for playing an active brotherly role in my life. But I'm sure Lamar thinks that I would definitely call on him first if I was ever in need of anything, and he's right, I would call him in most situations.

But Chris is my connection because I know that I've had a few encounters where I've come close to needing some help in getting away from Lamar when he's mad. But I've just been able to handle things on my own and correct the situations before letting them escalate into me having to call upon Chris to come and actually see him for real.

Ultimately, I know that Lamar would never hurt me or my girls, but he can be a very vicious man at times, and in some cases that within itself can be hazardous to him and to those of us closest to him.

But his good kind of outweighs his badness, so I'm going to stay with him and hopefully work out the problems within our relationship.

As for now, I turn to Lamar with a kiss and say. "I think we should wait to finish our conversation later because you know that we're not going to be able to finish talking about this out here."

"The most important stuff has been said already, so whatever we talk about after this can't top that news anyway."

"Is everybody ready to play volleyball?"

Chris yells out.

"And the losers have to do whatever the winners tell them to do for an hour!"

And everyone likes that idea so we all gather to get the game going. — We play men against the women until the security people finally come with the food that we ordered.

And after having to play two games due to everyone cheating on the first one, but we get out of the pool and we women have to do whatever the men tell us to do for an hour.

And surprisingly no one takes it too far with their demands by asking us to do anything crazy, I guess bossing us around like we're at their beck and call for absolutely everything is enough for them.

"So, what do you think we should do about our newly found female friends?"

I ask Sky when she comes to sit next to me chewing on something that she just got from the security house lady who came with the guys who brought the food.

"I'm still ready to slap the shit out of them!"

She shouts out loudly enough for them to hear her even if they aren't listening.

"Slapping them won't do nothing!" I shout back as we both laugh at how much we can tell that she's getting on my nerves. But I now redirect my attention to Lamar, who is chugging more drinks. So I ask Sky to hold on for a minute while I go over and interfere with him and all of that drinking.

Knowing that one out of two things is about to happen, he's going to go straight to sleep, or he'll be clinging to me like a moth to a flame all night until I allow him to fuck us both to sleep.

So I walk over to him. "So it looks like it's going to be another one of those nights huh, Lamar?"

"Yeah baby, I just hope that I don't hurt you again."

He replies while nodding his head yes with a freaky look on his face. But I just turn around and walk away without taking his drink as he get a good back view of what he's about to get.

And there are no words to explain his physical reactions during sex when he's full of alcohol. He becomes another person, and sometimes that's a good thing, and sometimes it's bad because he damn near hurt my back the last time he over drank.

Which is weird because it was during a real slow grind type of sex night; nothing was too fast or too rough, everything was slow and hard; but I guess it was a little too hard.

And Sky has now gotten up and moved by the time I make it back to my seat, so I take a detour and just head over to speak with our two new sneaky travel guests by myself.

"Hey ladies, we've been having so much fun, but I haven't said your names much because I'm bad with names. But my name is Chase Jordan, but of course, everybody calls me CJ. And since we're going to be out here together for so long, I figured I should formally reintroduce myself so that we can all get to know each other better."

I stand in front of them smiling, as if I don't know what they're all about. But out of nowhere, Sky comes walking up on us to listen to what I'm saying to them, but her face isn't wearing a smile.

And I know that Sky is a true friend to me, and she would help me fight or make peace or whatever it is that needs to be done at any time. But these two chicks have truly rubbed her the wrong way because she's never been this adamant about making sure that we handle any females due to a man, and I mean never.

And now I'm starting to let the situation bother me because of how much it's bothering her, because her abrupt presence is now telling me that somebody is about to get fucked up.

And if we're going to save this trip with some adult type of reasoning, then I'd better think of something really quick because with her already being annoyed and irritated, which now has me feeling annoyed and irritated with them even more at this point. I'm afraid that her earlier prediction of this not being such a good trip after all is about to come true, so I have to do something to soften the airwaves. — But these chicks have to know that something isn't right about our presence, it's beginning to reek of animosity.

But the light-skinned one still responds. "Hi CJ, I'm Tori, and this is my god-sister, Nina."

But before I can respond to her, Chris walks over to us and says to me. "I need to tell you something really important right now, Chase, so come and take a walk with me outside for a minute."

And everything about his presence catch not only me, but also Sky off guard because just like Sky. His demeanor is clearly agitated as well, and as I'm about to ask him what's wrong with him, he quickly interrupts me.

"Right now, CJ, we need to talk right now for real."

"What's wrong?" Sky asks him. "Is everything OK?"

And he doesn't give her a response, so now my mind goes from greeting Tori and Nina, to being totally concerned about Chris. Especially after all of the laughing and playing that we just did in the pool.

I'm totally alarmed by his actions, so without another thought I turn and walk away from Tori and Nina like they no longer exist, to go and see what's going on with Chris.

He now tells me that he just told Kris that he received an emergency call from his brother about something regarding me that didn't sound too good.

"I told her that I need to take a walk and talk with you about it before I say anything to anybody about it. So you can tell Lamar the same thing, unless you need for me to tell him for you."

He says while staring at me and moving his head up and down as if he's answering yes to a question.

"Okay Chris, but before I tell Lamar anything, I want to know what your brother said? And which brother was it?"

"I haven't talked to any of my brothers today, other than the one who's out here with us right now."

Staring even harder at me, he says. "I heard you telling Lamar that it looks like it's going to be another one of those nights. Then I heard him tell you that he hopes that he don't hurt you again, and I keep trying to block out everything that I'm hearing but I can't. All I can hear is the shit that y'all been saying to each other, so we need to talk, while you're out here talking about tasting like a piece of motherfucking candy."

He now has a frown on his face while looking at me sideways like he's really having some major issues with me and Lamar all of a sudden.

"Chris, are you being for real right now? Why are you repeating everything that he and I have said to each other? And you're seriously mad about it?"

Shaken and confused, I take a few steps back to get a better view of him for more answers. But his eyes are saying a million words as I place my hands on my hips and prepare myself to hear him explain himself.

But if body language and uneasy eyes could physically speak right now, his is saying that he's about to snap and fuck somebody up.

So instead of continuing to seek immediate information from him, I tell him that I'll go and talk to Lamar myself because this is just all too bizarre right now.

I quickly walk away from him to go and speak with Lamar, who's just about to sit down and eat, which is good because he won't care what I'm about to do while he's eating.

"Lamar, Chris just received a message that has him real uneasy right now, so I'm about to step outside and talk to him because he's tripping."

"All right, baby."

He says while eating some of his food. "Go handle your business and let me know if y'all need me."

"Okay, I will."

I now hurry back to go and find Chris, but he must have already gone outside because he is nowhere to be found.

So I go outside to look for him.

CHAPTER 9
"WHO DO YOU LOVE"

Although the sun isn't as bright as it was earlier, it's still beautiful outside, and it feels wonderful. And when I see Chris, he says that we should walk down to the small wooded supply house that's not far from the cabin.

"Everybody can still see us through those big windows if they want to."

He says as we begin to walk towards the small wooded house. "But they're all too busy eating to pay us any attention right now."

"I don't care if they can see us or not, Chris, it doesn't matter to me."

I get straight to the point. "What matters is that we discuss why were you repeating everything that Lamar and I have been saying to each other like that? I mean I'm almost at a loss for words because I don't get it, so what's up with you?"

"Look, CJ, I know that you're about to get upset at what I'm about to say to you, but fuck it. Because if I hear Lamar make one more comment about fucking you, then I'm going to lose my motherfucking mind anyway."

He says aggressively, yet still in somewhat of a calm tone.

"So we need to discuss our relationship again because I'm not as cool with all of this like I was at first."

"I'm truly at a loss for words because I really thought that we were beyond all of that, Chris. And if we weren't, why haven't you said anything to me before now?"

He now pulls my towel, gesturing for us to keep walking, but now looking as if he just lost his best friend or something.

"I tried to stop thinking about you in that type of way, but I'm in love with you. And it's not in a brotherly type of way, because I want to be with you in every way. And I know how bad this sounds, but if I continue to hold in how I feel about him touching you, then it's only going to get worse. And trust me, nobody wants that, not even me. So we need to figure this out."

Speechless, I stare at him and remain quiet and just keep walking, while feeling a little nervous and concerned about what would happen if Lamar actually heard him saying this to me right now.

"Say something, CJ, I can see it in your face that you're either confused or just mad. And I'm sorry about feeling this way, but it is what it is, so what's up?"

"What do you mean what's up, this isn't good! I have no idea what to say because I'm both mad and confused because you know that I love you, too! But I wasn't gearing my love towards that kind of love, and neither were you because you've never said or tried anything that would make me even think that. Nor have you tried anything sexually with me since that one night, so you tell me what's up? Furthermore, you know how I feel about Lamar. Just like I thought I knew how you felt about Kris, but now you've got my mind just swerving all out of control!"

"Listen, all I can say is that I'm sorry because it's a tough situation, CJ. But what else am I supposed to do besides tell you the truth, since I can't help how I feel?"

"I don't know what you're supposed to do, but you should have said something to me before now! So I guess I should let you know that before we came out here, Kris told me that something was bothering you because you've been acting distant towards her lately. And I know it's true because I saw you with my own eyes the other day at the shop, and if this is your reason for being so distant towards her, then we're about to have some serious problems. Because she's definitely going to think that we've had something going on this whole time, and so will Lamar."

"I'm not trying to start no trouble, but you know me better than anyone else out here. And if I'm paying this much attention to y'all, then you know that something has to change. And I know that I didn't say anything to you earlier, but I'm saying something to you now, so let's figure something's out because I didn't pay for this place to come and watch him have his way with you in front of my face."

"First of all, listen to how you sound, Chris. You know how things have been with me and Lamar all this time, so if we're bothering you this much then you've been feeling this way for a while. I mean really, I just don't understand why would you let all of us come way out here like this? And I thought the cabin was free for everybody this year?"

"I can pretty much run this place like it's mine, and the owners will agree, but it's never completely free at any time. I just didn't want nobody having to pay this year because I knew that Kris was coming. And she's going to fuck this trip up if things don't go her way, because I've already told her that I'm done with trying to have a relationship with her, as far as us being a couple is concerned. But she just won't let it go no matter how bad things get, so if anybody does get bothered by the peace disturbance that I know that she'll be in charge of. I figured they'll be okay because nobody had to pay to come anyway.

And I didn't mind paying for everybody to come because I was just ready to be stuck out here with you for the next five days. But I can't do it, I had to say something before I'm the one who's causing the disturbance instead of Kris. My only concern now is if you feel the same way about me, because I really am in love with you."

Shaking my head while feeling awkward and nervous about the fact that he's had my heart for quite some time now. But it's not his heart to have romantically with me still being involved with Lamar, so the only thing that keeps popping into my mind is that he should have said something to me before now.

"And I heard Yomme's lil chick telling Lamar that his shorts was puffy in the middle earlier, and he was grinning at her like he was enjoying how she was talking to him. So ya boy might be a little shady, before you think it's all good between y'all and try to rule me out."

He says as we continue towards the small wooded house.

"And I saw him take a piece of ice out of his cup and drop it down the front of her shirt. And then he said something about her nipples, now what does that tell you? And I could have fucked him up for that bullshit, but that's your man, right?"

"What do you want me to say, Chris? You're the second person who's told me something about this chick and Lamar, so I guess he's not my man. Especially if he's dropping ice down her shirt with puffy shorts and shit, but you know that you should have told me how you really felt about me before we all came out here together."

"I'm sorry for not telling you, but I'm telling you now. And at the end of the day, I believe that you feel the same way about me. And I did think about telling you a few times before now, but I knew that you would get mad at me now that you and Kris can finally get along. So I just kept it to myself, well, I told Markus. But that's as far as I went with it."

"I love you too, Chris, and you really do already know how much. But your timing couldn't be worse, and we said that we'd never revisit these emotions again to protect our friendship. And now my feelings are on a rampage with you and Lamar, because I'm pissed off that he's been flirting with this chick Tori behind my back like that. And I'm upset with you about how you've been keeping things from me like you've been doing lately."

"At first that was the reason why I hid the way I felt, because we said that we would never revisit those feelings again, because neither one of us was ready for it. But we're ready now, and as you can see, Lamar is not the one that you need to be claiming. So what's going to happen now?"

"With all of these surprises, I don't know what's next for you or for me. What I do know is that whether Lamar likes Tori or not, we have to keep what we're talking about to ourselves until I can figure something out. Because I just told Lamar that we can get back together when we were in the pool, and although he's in for a rude awakening if he ever tries to touch me again. Chris, you still can't be getting upset if you see his hands on me and flip out because I can handle it myself."

"OK, but that's why we're out here talking about it right now, because I'm going to say something if you keep letting him touch you. And I know this is all so sudden or whatever, but I haven't done anything sexual with Kris in a long time. So it's hard sitting around watching y'all make fuck faces at each other when I feel the way that I feel."

"Oh, whatever, Chris. We haven't been making any fuck faces at each other. But you definitely don't have to worry about any kind of fucking going on between us now, because he's officially off of my to-do list for real."

"Well, I know that you being in that swimsuit isn't helping me at all either." He says while looking me over and licking his lips as if he's tasting me within his thoughts or something.

"You know how I feel about you, Chris, but if we hook up right now then it would just be wrong on all levels. So please just stop looking at me like that."

And just as I'm heading in the right direction of turning things down, my body isn't agreeing with my thoughts of how this would still never work out for us. Because I don't reject him at all when he turns around to look back at the cabin, and then quickly pulls me behind the small wooded house and kisses me with enough passion to please a nation.

"I'm sorry," is all that I can hear him saying as he pulls me even closer to him while gripping my booty as the kiss continues.

And there is no more control over our emotions at this point because I'm not stopping him because I want more, and although I'm worried, I'm glad that we're not stopping.

"What about Lamar and Kris?" I whisper to him passionately.

"She can't get me like this," he says while breathing down my neck and kissing my ear while taking my hand and placing it on his thick penis. And I squeeze it and immediately think about letting it go as a brief moment of stopping myself just because it's the right thing to do pops into my head.

But it's truly too late to turn back now because he's already taken me back to our one-night stand of passion all over again. And now the only thoughts spiraling in my brain while squeezing his penis that was so popular back then, are the thoughts of him still having the biggest penis that I've ever had. Which is why I understood what the fuss was all about when some of those women were jealous of Kris, because they knew what she was getting whenever she wanted it. But now, although he keeps apologizing to me for what's happening; neither of us are honestly trying to stop it from happening. Not even to check to see if someone is coming to check on us now that I've let my towel come all the way unraveled and dropped to the ground, we do not care to check on anything.

We now lean against the house as he begins to rub his large erect penis against my vagina as best as he can with our height difference.

"I gotta have you now, Chase."

He grabs me and pulls me to the ground and onto my towel. While aggressively pulling my bikini bottoms to the side as he attacks my pussy with his mouth while quivering like a drug addict in need of a fix.

Now my nipples are standing at attention from wanting more of him because his cravings for me are so real, and I can feel it. And now so are mine for him, so of course I'm spreading my legs and giving him whatever he wants at this point.

Although my heart is starting to beat faster now that the flashbacks of how sensual he was is taking over my brain.

And how he would often forget how big he is when he laid into me that night of our one night stand. But I must have loved that passion because I desperately want those very same feelings to happen all over again right now.

And he obviously can tell by how I'm now all over him, but this situation isn't all the cool because a part of me really is feeling kind of guilty and thinking that this is just not the time or the place for this to happen.

"It's going down!"

He yells as we both burst into laughter, knowing that he and I are the type that will have sex just about anywhere.

"Oh my goodness, but we just can't do it right now, Chris! For real, wait! We have to be careful and just wait!"

I now pull back while trying to catch my breath and sticking my head around the corner, hoping that no one is coming to look for us.

"If its pain that you want, then I know that he can't bring it like I can." He says boastfully, as we both stand to our feet.

"What are you talking about—pain?"

"I'm not stupid, Chase."

He says, "I know what Lamar meant when he said that he hopes that he don't hurt you again."

And he doesn't seem to feel ashamed at all about sounding like a first-class stalker, by continuing to repeat things that Lamar and I have said to each other since we've been here.

"Seriously, Chris, I just can't believe that you've been listening to us like that!"

"I can't either, but I have, so who's it going to be?"

"Now what kind of fucked-up-ass question is that for you to ask me right now? Apparently we have everything in common including our best sex, but I still don't want to risk losing my very best male friend over trying to seriously have a romantic relationship with you that may not even work. So you shouldn't ask that question because you know that Kris and Lamar would never leave us alone if we ever get together like that for real, they'll constantly bring us hell. So let's just head back to the cabin and straighten all of this out later, after we've had time to process everything."

I now reach down to pick up my towel, thinking that I'm about to wrap it back around my body.

But with the lack of sex that he's had to deal with due to his feelings for me, it's overpowering his body because he acts like I haven't said anything and grabs onto me again.

And he's not only kissing me but also cuffing my breast and moaning like he's in heat, and I refuse to let him suffer regardless of my fears, so I reach down to pull his penis back out. Because dropping to my knees seems to be just what he needs in order for him to get some quick relief without us actually having sex, but his phone rings just as I snatch his shorts down and push him against the wooded house. — And his phone scares the shit out of me because for some reason, I just know that it's Kris or somebody calling from the cabin.

"See, Chris, we need to wait."

I suggest as the reality of how much we really do need to wait before doing this again starts to really sink in.

"Fuck that, CJ, they can wait!"

He says while we both can see that it's Markus's cell phone that's calling him.

Meaning that I was right, and they may be looking for us, so we do need to head back before Lamar comes walking out here looking for me since I don't have my phone with me.

"I'm sorry, but we have to wait, Chris. Let's just head back because we can handle all of this later, I'm getting too nervous."

"We can head back but we need to figure something out right now, not later. How about we get together in about thirty minutes or so and try to figure it out some kind of way?"

"I don't know, let's just take it one moment at a time until we can get things situated. And what should I tell Kris when she asks me what's going on? Because you know that she's going to ask me about it as soon as she sees me."

"I don't know, tell her whatever you want to tell her. Kris is just going to have to accept it one way or another, just like Lamar will. And you may think that he's going to be a big problem for us, but he won't be. I'm not worried about him and neither should you be worried because he's not a fool."

He says without a care in the world, like he doesn't know that Lamar is just as crazy as he is.

But as we now decide to walk back to the cabin, I reiterate.

"Just remember not to start anything with Lamar, please, just let me handle that whole thing by myself. OK?"

"Okay, handle it. But let's link up later in about half an hour."

Again he calmly and nonchalantly tries to hook up with me, like he doesn't care that this is wrong.

"You are just too calm right now when this is a very serious matter, Chris, and somebody really could get hurt!"

"I'm not calm, I'm just confident, and I don't want you to keep worrying about Kris and Lamar because I'll handle them. You'll see."

"I know I'll see, and that's why we need to wait until we can talk and get things situated before we go any farther with this. Because we've shared a lot of our thoughts, feelings, and so much more for years. But I've never asked you about the rumors of how notorious you were back in the day. And that was because I honestly didn't want to know, because I love who you are now, even Lamar knows that because I talk to him all the time by using your life as an example of how he can change his lifestyle before something crazy happens."

I continue as we head back.

"And when I bring up your past to Lamar, he really does see how he can have a positive change like yours when he's ready, but that's the only time that I ever really bring up your past at all. So it really didn't matter to me how notorious you were, because you're not like that anymore. But if we decide to go farther with a romantic relationship for real, then you have to kill the rumors and tell me about yourself. Because with everything that I know about you, you know that there's a ton of stuff that I'm completely in the dark about. But that's about to change because I need to know so that I can be in chill mode like you are right now."

"I'll tell you whatever you want to know, we'll have time to talk about all of that later because you know that I trust you. The only reason that you don't know already is because you never wanted to know, and I understood why."

"Well, I heard that you had people running drugs and stuff for you, and Sky told me that she heard that you went somewhere and literally came back with a million dollars. And I can remember when we were teens, I never really saw you much until we got older, and as adults we were so on and off because you kept moving around so much with and without your brothers that I didn't know what to believe. But I knew that some of that stuff was true, but then when we started back getting close and really connecting and staying close. I knew that you were legally legit and about your business regardless of how you got there. So I never cared to dig farther into it until now, and I'm not going to lie, I'm a little scared."

"Scared of what?"

He says. "You know what, don't answer that. I got you, Chase. And I'm going to fill you in on whatever you want to know about me when we hook back up."

"Okay, but I'm still not sure about this."

"I understand that. But trust me, we'll be okay."

CHAPTER 10
"TOO MANY SECRETS"

I head for the bathroom to wash my hands, so that I can eat when Chris and I make it back to the cabin. And Sky rushes over to me and says that she's coming into the bathroom with me because she wants to know what's going on.

"So, what's going on with Chris? And does it have anything to do with why Kris and Markus were arguing while y'all were outside?"

"I didn't know that Kris and Markus were arguing while we were outside. What happened?"

"I don't know. I thought that's what Chris was out there talking to you about. All I heard was them yelling at each other, but I couldn't make out what they were saying before it got quiet. The fuss ended in the bedroom, but it got started in one of these other rooms."

"Kris and Markus could have been arguing about how she's been feeling lately, but he can't help her because Chris just told me that he's in love with me, and that he don't want me to be with Lamar anymore."

"What?"

79

She yells. "Oh my God, are you serious?"

"Yes, I'm serious. That's why he needed to talk to me because he was getting upset with how Lamar and I were all over each other earlier. He said that if he hear Lamar say one more thing about fucking me, then he's going to go crazy on somebody."

Her mouth now falls open just as mine did after being stunned by his sudden news of affection.

But after pausing for a moment, her questions begin.

"Where did all of that come from? And what else did he say?"

"Basically that's it, he said that he's in love with me and that he want us to get together and officially become a couple for real. And he also told me that he's already told Markus how he feels about me, that's why I'm curious about the argument between Kris and Markus. Although he did say that Kris has no idea of how he really feels about anything or anybody besides her, so I'm really not sure of exactly what's going on right now. But I know that if she knew, then she would've said something to me or him by now. Especially after he told me that she's going to try to do all that she can to mess up this trip if things don't go her way. So I think that Kris may just want some answers, and Markus just can't give them to her, so she could have been arguing with him about damn near anything at this point."

"Okay, but CJ what I want to know is what did you say to Chris after he told you how he was feeling about you?"

"At first, I did exactly what you just did—my mouth fell open because he totally caught me off guard. Because I had no idea, I mean I know that he loves me and everything, but I didn't know that it was all like that."

"Girl, that's wild, so what are y'all going to do about it now? And how do you feel about him?"

"You already know how I feel about him, but I don't know what I'm going to do about all of this just yet." I now shake my head while drying my hands and looking at her like I'm all confused.

"There's actually a little more to me and Chris that you don't know about, Sky. We had sex a few years ago, but we agreed to never bring it up again after it happened."

"What? Oh Lord, I can't take it!"

She shouts. "You and Chris this whole time, and you haven't said anything to me about it!"

"I've never said anything about it because it was a onetime-only thing that I was going to take to my grave, especially since we have managed to stay close friends without that type of attachment after we did it."

"Okay, so how long is a few years ago, CJ? And I should have known that y'all had something going on this whole time other than just being 'best friends'!"

She uses her fingers as quotation marks when she says "best friends".

"We haven't had anything going on this whole time besides what you already know about, and that's for real."

I say as convincingly as I can. "It seriously only happened one time, and I know that it's a little suspect that we hid it. But we get along so well as friends that we just didn't want to mess everything up by talking about it or involving anybody else. Because we knew that neither one of us was ready for a relationship at the time, so I figured there was no need to say anything about it until now."

Still shaking her head she says. "And you're the one who's always saying—what's in secret will eventually come to light!"

"I know, and this light is bright because when we were outside we kissed. And girl, I wanted to break down and cry because it felt so damn good, although I know that all hell is about to break loose because I knew that I loved him. But I didn't know how much until now, because if I have to choose between him and Lamar, then I'm choosing Chris because while we were airing out our secrets. He told me that he heard Tori telling

Lamar that his shorts was puffy in the middle. And that Lamar just laughed at her when she said it, and then he took a piece of ice out of his cup and dropped it down the front of her shirt, and then he said something about her nipples."

"Damn! So her and Lamar been doing it like that, huh?"

Sky roars. "I told you that these bitches are out here and up to no good, didn't I? Oh it's on now for real, they're about to get their asses beat like they done stole something for this bullshit! And you and Chris got busy more than just that one time, too. Because if y'all are thinking about getting serious like that, then something more has been going on than just that one-night stand. I know better than to believe that shit, just like I know that I'm ready to go back in here and handle these bitches."

"I told you that we're going to get them, but just give me a little while longer, Sky. For real, because you're right—their asses are as good as got even more now, I promise you that. And I knew that you weren't going to believe me when I said that Chris and I hooked up only that one time, but on everything it's the truth. Why wouldn't I just go ahead and admit everything to you right now if we've really been getting together like that this whole time? I seriously would just go ahead and tell you right now, but that's just not the case."

She now walks over to the sink to wash her hands and says. "Nah, I believe you. But for real, though, it's going to be tragic if Lamar finds out that you and Chris got together like that at all! And it doesn't matter if y'all did it before or after he met you, the point is that it happened. And on top of that, if Kris finds out, you know that she'll turn stupid crazy."

"I would like to think that I can keep him and her on ice until I can figure out what's really happening between me and Chris right now. I just need to sit down and have a serious conversation with him first, because this is a lot to take in."

"Yep, it's a lot."

She says. "But CJ, Lamar is on my shit list for touching or even talking to this chick out here, for real. So his ass deserves whatever he's got coming to him for flirting with her, and I know that he better not come to me begging, talking about Sky please talk to Chase for me. Because I'm not, and when you and Chris went outside, I was watching y'all from the window at first. But when I walked away from the window, Nina walked past me and Chad, but I didn't see Tori. But I'm sure she's somewhere around here plotting with her whorish ass."

"Yeah, but Tori is not a factor to me right now. I'm more worried about me, Chris, Kris, and Lamar. Even though I shouldn't be because Lamar has already fucked up with me for the last time in a major way, and I wish that I could just go in there and straight tell him how I feel about Chris, since he can't keep his hands to himself. But Chris and I got together before me and Lamar even knew each other, and he really have been nothing but a platonic friend to me this whole time for real. But I know that it would still hurt Lamar. But going at him with this kind of information out here is just a disaster waiting to happen because it would hurt him and Kris. Although I can handle Kris all by myself if she gets stupid, but I can't control Lamar or Chris if they get mad at each other."

"I bet you're ready to go home already, aren't you?"

Sky asks while seeing the frustration in my face, as she now gives me a big bear hug after drying her hands.

"Thanks, because I need some comfort right now for real."

I now rest my head on her shoulder and answer her question. "But no, I'm not ready to go home under these circumstances. You know that Chris is like an uncle to my girls, and I don't want us to be acting different around them until we know exactly what's what between us. But before I leave here, I'm going to decide if I'm still single, or if Chris and I really are leaning towards taking things farther without a doubt about it."

"I can't believe Chris after all this time is just now opening up like that out of the clear blue sky, CJ. Are you sure that you didn't know that he liked you before now? Because y'all do play around a lot, and you should have known that y'all wasn't going to be able to just have sex and ignore it like it never happened. Because honestly, both of y'all have always been a little suspect in that area, so I won't judge you if you tell me that y'all really have been banging each other this whole time. Because I kind of already knew it deep down inside of my brain." She says while smiling at me like she's guessed it all right again.

"I mean, a part of me honestly believes you, but a part of me honestly don't."

"Well, I'm telling you the truth. It only happened once, and I really didn't know that he felt this way about me until today. Like I said, I knew that he had love for me. But having love for someone and being in love with them are two totally different types of love."

"I actually think that you and Chris will make just as good of a match as you and Lamar did, but I'm telling you right now that neither Kris nor Lamar will ever leave y'all alone. No matter how many people can already tell that y'all have way more feelings for each other than y'all would ever admit to. And I'm sure that Kris and Lamar can probably see it just as much as we see it, but they still aren't going to go for y'all having that type of relationship. Somebody will get hurt if y'all actually start admitting it, because it's really always been quite obvious."

"Nobody can tell that we have more feelings than we were admitting to because I've never openly showed those kinds of feelings towards Chris in public. Seriously, I would never even think of showing that kind of interest in him around anybody, including you. So I think that it'll be a shock to everybody just like it was a shock to you, for real."

"Maybe you think that it'll be a shocker because in your mind you were trying to bury how you really felt at times, but I'm not shocked. I'm surprised because it's unexpected, and of course at first I appeared to be shocked because it's actually true. But now that I know, I don't think that many people will be as shocked as you think they'll be. Because I noticed you and Chris myself last year a few days before your birthday, when you and Lamar had gotten arrested for those traffic tickets."

"You noticed what?"

"I noticed that when we came and got you out of jail that night, he was talking to you like he was your man. I was on my phone but I still heard y'all talking, but I just didn't say anything because y'all were arguing like he'd caught you cheating on him or something. Like for real, but I also figured that maybe he really did just care about your well-being in that situation. So I just overlooked it because he had a right to be mad at you that night. Because if the police would've known that they could have arrested you for more than just a damn traffic ticket, then you would have had way more charges added for pulling a stunt like that for Lamar and his dumb ass cousin. So honestly, I didn't really believe the hype for real every time you would say ugh, when somebody asked you if you could ever be with Chris like that. I knew that every time you said 'ugh', it was some 'ugh', bullshit, and you liked him for real."

And as Sky continues to talk, my mind is now stuck looking back on my birthday last year, when Lamar and I got arrested. And the continued spiral of disappointments concerning drugs that I've had to deal with while being in a relationship with him. Although that particular incident wasn't his fault, because Lamar had been treating me all week for my birthday, and then three days before the actual date of my birthday. His cousin Chewy, who doesn't drink or smoke, became our designated driver for the day.

Because Lamar and I had started drinking early, so we were already tipsy, and I was having the time of my life until we found out that Chewy was free of drugs and alcohol within his body. But he had some meth, pills, and eight rocks of cocaine in the car with us.

But being totally unaware of the fact that he had drugs in the car, Lamar and I allowed him to drive us everywhere like he was our chauffeur. And he knew that Lamar would never travel with any type of drugs in a car with him at all, nor would he ever have me in the car with anything without telling me first. But that asshole was intending to sell it to some guy at the party that he was taking us to.

And he was just freely driving us around like nothing could happen to him for driving on a suspended license, and with drugs in the car, but that's kind of our own fault because all we knew was that he didn't drink or smoke.

We just assumed that everything else was all good without asking him if he was really legit or not.

But the moment he sped through a yellow light while trying to catch it before it turned red, I quickly saw that his cousin wasn't the person that I thought he was.

We heard the sirens of a police car coming straight for us, and that's when Chewy nervously told us about the meth, pills, and cocaine. Along with him having a warrant, and not having a valid driver's license.

Then he suggested that he should try to outrun the police, because he didn't want to go back to jail. But Lamar told him that if he didn't pull the car over, then he wouldn't live another day to outrun the police or anybody else for running with us in the car with him, whether we got locked up or not. He told him that he would die in jail or in these streets if he did anything stupid. And then Lamar told me that the police would be asking us who we are because when they run Chewy's name.

And see that he has a warrant out for him, then one of us was probably going to have to drive, or maybe they'll take the car.

Then he crushed everything when he told me that they were going to arrest him, too, because there was a warrant out for him as well.

He said that it wasn't for anything major, but he knew that there could possibly be a warrant out for his arrest too. So he had gotten on the phone and had somebody to call his lawyer because he couldn't get him on the phone right then. And that's when Chewy told us that he thinks that he may have two warrants out for his arrest, but he wasn't sure about it, and we could immediately see that we would have been better off just taking our chances and driving ourselves to the party.

Because all I could think of was if the police find those drugs in the car, then we all might go to jail. But I didn't get too nervous because I knew that the drugs wasn't ours, and that after whatever that was about to happen, Lamar was still going to fuck Chewy up for putting us in that situation anyway.

So when he slowly pulled the car over, Chewy started suggesting all kinds of crazy shit like if the cops find anything, then we should say that we didn't have any drugs; and that they planted them.

And I was just so done with him at that point, and Lamar was so mad that he could have spit fire. But we didn't have time for Lamar's threats of harming Chewy if he didn't let them know that those were his drugs. Because Chewy must have been on some kind of drugs after all because he was acting like he wasn't scared of Lamar. And I honestly thought that his snake ass were still going to say that the drugs weren't his, so I just took matters into my own hands. I was the only one who didn't have any warrants or prior offenses, so I figured that they wouldn't do very much to me besides ask me my name. And as long as the cop didn't have a K-9 present or anything like that, then I would be fine if I decided to stick the drugs between my legs. I was basically only thinking about Lamar and the strong possibility of Chewy not taking ownership of his drugs if the car is searched.

And since I was on the last day of my menstrual cycle, and I just so happened to have on a maxi pad that night.

I told Chewy to pass me the drugs after I'd picked up a napkin that was in the back seat with us, and then I wrapped the meth, pills, and rocks tightly inside of the napkin and squeezed it. Compressing it all together inside of my fist, then I unzipped my jeans and stuck the wrapped drugs inside of my panties. Snugging it between my vagina and the pad tightly enough so that if I were searched, the drugs would still be hidden.

Although I was hoping that the cop wouldn't notice anything suspicious enough for him or her to even search us at all, but they did have warrants out for them, so there was no telling what could happen. And I was going to dispose myself of everything after the cops took them away and let me go.

But when the officer approached the car, he said that he pulled us over to let Chewy know that his left brake light was blown, and that he should slow down at yellow lights and not just speed through them like that. Because the light had actually turned red, so he should've just stopped.

But the officer still decided to ask him for his license and insurance information, but Chewy couldn't produce neither. And everything just went downhill after that because he went to jail, Lamar went to jail, and so did I.

They said that I had received two separate tickets that was never taken care of, one from a traffic violation. And one from being illegally parked somewhere, he said that I had even been notified through the mail a few times. But neither has been taken care of, and I told him that was because it was probably mailed to the address that my car is registered to.

And that's my mom's address, but I was never given any mail concerning any kind of traffic or parking tickets. So I was shocked that I had a warrant out for me, and upset that I was hauled away with meth, pills, and cocaine stuffed between my padded pussy.

And it's safe to say that I was nervous because there wasn't anything that Lamar, Chewy, or anyone else could do to help me when they cuffed me and put me in the backseat of that police car.

But after I was booked and fingerprinted, I told the female officer who took my picture that I was on my menstrual cycle, and I really needed to go to the restroom.

And at first, she told me to just hold it and I can use the toilet when I get in a cell. But thankfully, after making me wait until she completed all of her paperwork, she gave me a fresh pad and actually led me to a restroom.

Where I dropped the wrapped drugs into the toilet and flushed them until there was nothing left, which took only one flush, but I flushed it again just to make sure that everything was gone.

And when Chris came with Sky to get me out of jail, I told them what all had happened as soon as we got on the interstate to go home. And Chris was extremely mad at me for taking such a risk, and even more mad at Lamar for allowing me to do it.

"Okay, so now what should we do or say when we leave this bathroom?"

Sky says. "Because I really don't know how to act once we walk out of here."

"Just do the best that you can to keep everything together, because Chris said that he's going to try to be cool and let me handle things now that he's talked to me about it. And your ass can stop playing with me about us hiding it. Because Sky, it seems like Chris really have been holding in a lot, and now he's ready to pop and he don't care who knows about it. So I'm just hoping and praying that things don't get out of control for real, because I'll go in there and just lock myself in the bedroom and not come out until it's time to go back home."

Snickering at the thought of me actually going in there and locking myself away, we both just laugh while doing a mirror check before exiting the bathroom.

CHAPTER 11
"IT'S GOING DOWN"

As soon as I fix myself a plate and sit down to eat my food, the one person whom I don't want to converse with the most comes walking over to sit with me.

"CJ, I need to talk to you, but you have to keep eating and acting like we're just having a regular conversation." Kris says to me while taking a seat in front of me.

"No matter what I say to you, you have to keep eating and not get mad because if Markus sees me talking to you, and your expressions change. Then he's going to know that I opened my big-ass mouth, and I know that you're cool with me, but everybody else in Chris's family really don't like me as it is already. But I'm still going to tell you what happened anyway, regardless of how Markus feels."

Now looking around the room more than she's looking at me, she seems anxious. "Markus just had to force my fingers from Tori's short ass hair not too long ago, because I tried to pull her brains out with my bare hands."

"Why, Kris? What happened?"

"When you and Chris was outside, I had left my drink in that last room down the hallway. But when I finally thought to go back inside to get it, the door was locked. So I knocked on it until somebody opened it, because I could hear somebody in there talking, so I knew that the room wasn't empty. Then finally Tori came to open the door as soon as Markus came walking up behind me to go in there to get the lighter that he'd left in the ash tray. And when me and Markus were walking into the room, Lamar was walking out, then Tori was kneeling down to pick up a pile of coasters that she must have knocked over before she opened the door. But I didn't think anything of it at first, until Markus said that he had forgotten that these doors had locks on them. And that's when I asked Tori why was she and Lamar in there with the door locked? And the bitch got smart, saying that if that was any of my business, then she would have told me before I had left the room in the first place. So instantly and without a thought, I grabbed her by her throat with one hand, and by her hair with my other hand while I lifted my leg and tried to slam her head into my knee because I just snapped. I'm so tired of bitches getting smart for no reason."

And I want to stop Kris right now and ask her where everybody else was, because Sky surely didn't tell me anything about a fight. But this must have been what the ruckus was about that she heard between Kris and Markus, so I'm just going to sit quietly and let her finish.

She says. "Markus ran to lock the door back and then came and broke us up before telling us that if we didn't stop, he was going to choke the shit out of both of us. And he already had that slut by her neck because she was kicking and shit, but that didn't mean anything because I was trying to bust her shit wide open, just as much as I was trying to pull out every strain of hair left on her bald-ass head. Markus told her that whatever she and

Lamar had going on needed to stay in that room, but I told him and her that she can't keep shit in that room because I was going to tell you. But after she left the room, Markus told me not to say anything to you until we get back home. But I feel like that bitch needs to be choked out again with her smart-ass mouth."

And at this point, I'm not sure if Kris is really angry with Tori for being in there with Lamar, or if she's just completely fed up with smart-mouth women in general; and that's what really made her snap.

Regardless, I'm ready to blow a fuse right now just like she did, because this has taken another turn for the worse for me and Lamar. Although I do feel a little guilty because Kris is trying to be a friend to me by telling me this, when in reality. Whatever happened between Lamar and Tori couldn't have been any worse than what had just happened between me and Chris.

"I guess Markus is going to have to be mad at you after all, Kris, because I'm going to need to know why in the hell were they in that room with the door locked. They both got me so fucked up thinking that I'm Miss Boo-Boo the Fool or somebody, but watch me have the last laugh. Because you're not the first or the second person to come and tell me something about these two motherfuckers, and how they've been sneaking around behind my back. What you did do was only clarify everything that I've suspected, and made clear what's been told to me already."

"Well, I know that Chris just came to you with some shit, and now this. But I had to let you know about what happened, because it's fucked up how they think that they're so slick, and I felt like you should know."

"Wow, Kris, there's so much crap going on right now that I'm just at a loss for words."

I disclose while absorbing the news that she just gave me, while at the same time feeling stunned by how much she's changed.

And has seriously been trying to be a good friend to me, especially within these past few months. So this is making me feel horrible because we have truly overcome our differences, and now this.

She says. "I know that this is probably not the best time to be asking you this, but what's going on with what Chris needed to talk to you about? What's the matter?"

Awaiting an answer from me, she stares at me.

But I pause and try to dodge the question by getting up and preparing to walk away. "Let me go and put this food away and fix me a strong drink because I've completely lost my appetite, then maybe we can talk about it."

"Okay."

Now rushing to get away from the table and away from any conversations that have anything to do with me and Chris, I grab my food and water and get as far away from her as possible.

Lamar now sees me and grabs me from behind. "Two to one on the dartboard, baby!"

Jerking away from him, I yell. "Let me go, Lamar, with your snaky ass!"

Now looking at me all shocked like he hasn't done anything wrong, he says. "Damn, Chase, what's wrong with you?"

"Let's go to the bedroom, motherfucker, and I'll tell you exactly what the fuck is wrong with me! As if you don't already know!"

I can tell that he can immediately feel the tension in my voice, along with everyone else who can hear us. But he's still acting like he's lost as to why I'm so upset with him, while we now walk into the bedroom.

"So you're really going to try to fuck this bitch right in my face, Lamar? And you can stop acting like you don't know what the fuck I'm talking about, because all that's going to do is just piss me off even more!"

Switching gears, he shouts. "She keeps flirting with me and shit, but I'm not thinking about that broad CJ, you know that I don't want her! Why are you tripping like this?"

"Why in the hell were y'all in that room with the door locked?"

His words now begin to come out all tangled and twisted as he begins to answer my question.

But my anger temperature is now being turned up to burn and kill him as we both can plainly see that his stuttering means that he's obviously lying to me in my face. And he has me on flaming boil and ready to erupt on his ass because I constantly tell him all the time that I hate liars.

Although we all lie at some point or another, but he can clearly see that this is just not the time to be lying.

"Fuck you, Lamar, I told you that you wasn't ready for marriage or any of that bullshit that you claim that you're trying to have with me! Man, if I knew that I could get away with it, I would punch you in your motherfucking face right now!"

Happy, yet not so happy to be the victim at the moment. I just want to get away from him before I do actually end up heading to jail or to a hospital for real.

Because the fact that he's really stuttering and lying to me really does hurt my feelings, and I'm about to hit him for real.

"I told you that I don't want her, so you need to check that shit straight-up, Chase!"

"I hate liars, get out of my way, Lamar!"

I shove my way past him to snatch a sundress from the closet. And now as I try to leave the room, he pushes the door back to close it, and apparently thinks that I'm going to change my tone after he gets in my face. Talking loud like I will back down, he says. "I said that I don't want that bitch, so you might as well sit your ass down because you're not about to leave this room yet!"

"Lamar, I'm going to ask you one last time about what happened in that room, and if you look me in my face and lie to me again. You can do whatever you want to do to me right now because I'm going to be done with you forever for lying to my face like this. Seriously, you'll get more respect from the truth even if it hurts me. And you know that I'm going to find out what's going on anyway, so I don't know why you're standing here acting like nothing has happened besides flirting. Because I know better than that."

"I let her suck my dick, Chase."

He now pierce my ears with his raw and unadulterated truth.

"I tried to stop her at first, but I knew that she wasn't going to stop until I let her do what she do. But I promise you that I had already made her stop before Kris came and knocked on that door."

"Wow," I murmur while staring at him like he's a ghost.

"She's been trying to get my dick in her mouth ever since we got out here, so I just let her do it. But baby, I'm sorry. And I made her stop way before we heard them knocking—straight-up. I fucked up and I'm so sorry Chase, you gotta know that I don't want that hoe for real!"

He now begins to shout while clutching my arm really tight, although it's unnecessary for him to grab me because I can now barely move a muscle or say much of anything after hearing that she's already had her mouth on him for real. And that he actually allowed it to happen like I'm not out here with him.

Luckily, I'm not mad enough at him to start something that I may or may not can finish by actually hitting him in his face when I know that I'm just as guilty as he is. But I do need to leave and get away from him before I make something ignorant happen that I may or may not regret later by just flat-out telling him about me and Chris right now, so that I can slice his heart into little pieces just like mine is right now.

"My dick was barely even getting hard for her because I don't want her, so you have to forgive me! It's nothing for you to overreact about because I stopped her Chase, she was trying hard but I knew that I had already fucked up!"

I now know that I'm definitely going to fuck Chris with all of my might the first chance I get, regardless of if he could get hard for her or not, so I guess I have to forgive him.

"Regardless of what happened between y'all, Lamar, I'm done with this relationship for a while. Just move on, and we can still be friends because I can't even be mad at you because I knew that you weren't ready for a committed relationship anyway. And I've told you that several times, but now you should be able to see it for yourself, so just leave me alone."

Instantly we begin a major tug-of-war battle with the doorknob, but I know that he'll only go so far in trying to keep me in here with him because we're not out here alone.

So I end up winning the door battle as I'm now able to speed out of the room.

"CJ, I know I messed up, but just stop and listen to me!"

He shouts while rushing behind me after bursting through the door as we head down the hallway, passing Chris and Markus. But they grab Lamar and tell him to chill out, and just let me go and calm down.

"So you're just going to disrespect me in my—"

And before I can say face, I've already run up on Tori and thrown a punch with as much force behind it as I can when I see her standing by the front door looking stupid.

My fist met her nose as soon as I could get close to her, and then I hit her in her chin with my other fist.

And as she stumbles back to try to catch herself from falling, and to gather herself to swing back on me. Chris swoops me up from behind to take me outside, while leaving Markus and Chad to tend to Lamar.

Sky and Rayci comes running in from the patio, just as Yomme and Nina's boyfriend comes running in as well.

They all see Chris carrying me out, while Nina and Rayci is trying to get control of Tori, because she's now trying to come outside. While at the same time I'm trying to get back inside so that we can bang it out one on one because we're both furious and ready for whatever.

Especially me because I just know that she heard us in there screaming at each other about her whorish ass, and I really want to show her that I'm not playing with her for real.

And when I glance and see Yomme running in as I'm being carried out of the front door, he looks surprised and just as lost as I was before finding out the truth.

And when we get completely outside and away from everyone, Chris puts me down and tells me to calm down and quit sobbing over Lamar.

"I'm not sobbing over nobody! I'm just not about to be disrespected by him or anybody else out here!"

"OK, so calm your ass down if you're not sobbing over him!" He shouts as we walk towards the golf cart cars while Sky comes storming from the cabin saying.

"Where are y'all about to go? I'm going, too!"

The three of us now gets inside of the cart as Chris search for the keys, that he finds above his head.

And he drives off as soon as we see Lamar coming from the cabin with Markus and just about everybody else.

"I thought that you were going to wait before saying anything to him about her anyway?" Chris states as he speeds away before anyone can try to stop us.

"I tried to wait, but he let her suck his dick!"

"What?" Sky and Chris both voice at the same time.

"Exactly!" I express back while shaking my head with my eyes closed, to keep any tears that may form from falling.

Even though I'm just as guilty for falling for Chris, but my heart is still broken because Lamar really did betray me. But I don't want to wear my heart on my sleeve too much, especially in front of Chris right now, so I just keep my eyes closed and listen to them talk.

"That's some fucked-up shit for Lamar to do, and I should really go back there and fuck him up for real now, but I'd much rather go back and shake his hand because he just made it real clear that he's definitely not the one for you." Chris says to me, while now turning around to immediately look at Sky as he explains to her how everything is happening through some sort of divine intervention.

But Sky really isn't believing the whole divine intervention thing because she says. "I should have known that you and CJ had something else going on this whole time by the way y'all are always acting towards each other! Brother and sister my ass!"

"Nah, it wasn't like that. At first she was kind of like my little sister slash best friend."

"I told you!" I blurt out while opening my eyes to look back at her and join their conversation.

"But over the years one thing led to another as we got closer, and I just fell in love with her. And with everything in my heart, I know that outside of my mom, Chase is the only other woman who I can genuinely say that I love without a shadow of doubt. Even when I'm not tolerable, she knows just how to get me right without us having to do anything physical. She's a big part of my heart and I love her more than I can fully explain it."

"I told you!" I yell again.

But Sky says. "Whatever, Chase, don't try to act like y'all still didn't have a little something extra brewing! Because the physical sex may have happened just that one night, but y'all kept making love to each other emotionally!"

"I don't know what she's told you, but I can tell you that I love her just as much as she loves me, if not more."

He continues to talk to Sky, but now looks over at me and says. "So why not just make it happen, CJ? All we're missing now is just the physical stuff, and we both know that the physical stuff is the best stuff when we've already got everything else solidified, right? So let's make it happen, Captain."

"Dang, Chris, your love Jones is coming through all up front and personal today, huh! You're not playing with CJ, and that's what's up because you've even got me back here smiling by the way you want her. We all know how you feel about her anyway, but CJ, I bet you're already starting to feel better now after listening to him."

"Chris always makes me feel better, but that's not going to stop Lamar from getting into that other cart to come and follow us and break up all of this love. And like I said earlier, I don't want Chris and Lamar into it out here over this, so everything is fine now only for the moment. But what's going to happen when we have to come face-to-face with Lamar and his stubbornness?"

I now look around and try to think of what I should do if he really does come rolling up behind us in that other cart.

"I can go ahead and tell you now that it's not going to be easy for him to let you go. Especially since he knows that he fucked up, but I'm not going to interfere until you ask me to. Just don't ask me to interfere until you're real sure about it, because when I do step in then you're completely out of it. It'll be between me and him at that point, and he shouldn't have shit else to say to you once I'm involved. And I mean that shit."

Chris reassures me of his intentions of being his usual virile self, and I know how much of a reasonable person he is. Until he isn't, and he begins to talk like that. And with Lamar having such a similar personality, it scares me to my core because I know how they both are when it comes to proving themselves.

"I know that everything happens for a reason, but this is just all happening too fast."

"I know right!"

Sky says, "And I'm trying not to get all nervous like you are CJ, but we really can't help but to be nervous because we can't forget that Tori's boyfriend is probably back there asking her what's going on right about now. I'm sure he's asking her why were y'all fighting, and what if him and Lamar got into it after we left!"

"Tori and I didn't really get a chance to fight because Chris grabbed me and Nina grabbed her before we could really tussle. You just ran in on him carrying me out after I had confronted her and hit her in her face for disrespecting me, but we couldn't really get at each other after that because I was carried out."

"And Yomme is not tripping off of that girl like that." Chris chimes in, "Because he and his baby momma are still together. She's just his sidepiece, he don't really care about her for real, that's why he brought her way out here and away from everybody. So if he does trip off of anything, it'll probably be off of Lamar disrespecting him by letting her do that shit. But not because he loves her, he knows what she is."

"Man, I thought that she was his girlfriend!" Sky yells while mean mugging Chris like he's the one who brought her out here. "And why do men have to have a side chick with y'all shady asses? Why couldn't he just simply bring his baby momma with him? I'm sure she would've loved to come out here!"

"I don't need a side chick so don't be putting me in the same category with him, because I always keep it one hundred. Even when I was out here like that I never kept anyone in the dark about anything so that nobody could get upset, because I made it clear to everyone that I was single. And they all knew it until Kris came along, and I decided to change, and I've never cheated on Kris because she was enough for me. Even now while she thinks that I don't love her, I actually do love her. I'm just not in love with her because CJ has my whole heart, so I don't have anything to hide from nobody. But as far as this shit that's happening right now, all I'm saying is that Yomme won't be tripping off of Tori like you think he will. Now Lamar on the other hand—you may be right because that's some disrespectful shit."

He says while shaking his head. "But I don't think that they will fight, but whatever's going on back there. I'm sure that Chad and Markus have everything under control by now."

He now stops the cart and gets out. "So what do you want to do, Chase?"

"I don't know, but staying out here with all of this mess is not an option anymore. So I guess I'd better figure something out because somebody is going to have to leave, or else I'm going to leave."

I step out of the cart to join him and Sky, as she's gotten out as well.

"CJ, if you leave then I'm leaving, too!"

Sky says. "You're not about to leave me out here with them, so you might as well include me and Chad in your journey because we're leaving, too!"

"Nah, that's not going to happen."

Chris says. "If anyone is going to leave these grounds it'll be them, as a matter of fact. I'm about to go back so that I can personally escort her and Lamar's ass away from here. And I'm not going to say anything about me and Chase or disrespect nobody or none of that, I'm simply about to go back and tell them that they have to leave because we didn't come way out here for this shit."

Chris now walk to get back into the cart to leave, as if a light bulb has just been turned on inside of his head.

CHAPTER 12
"IT'S OVER"

We see Lamar, Chad, Kris, Markus, and Rayci all stuffed inside of the cart coming towards us.

And just as I suspected, Lamar doesn't hesitate when he sees us parked and about to get back into the cart with Chris to leave.

He jumps out and comes directly to me, asking to talk.

"I really need to holler at you for a minute, CJ, so let's just go somewhere and talk this shit out. I know that I fucked up, but I'll make it up to you straight-up, I promise you that shit will never ever happen again. They're back there packing their stuff so that they can head back to the city."

"Well, you need to head back to warn Tori not to go back home because her ass is as good as got when I get back home thanks to you! But you know what, Lamar? I think that you're expecting me to clown, but I'm going to do you one even better than that and just stop fucking with you forever! Fuck you and her!"

"We'll never stop fucking with each other forever so you can just kill that noise!" He shouts at me with an inkling of rage.

"Oh, it's a wrap, so all of that chasing can stop now because I'm over it! Fuck it, I'm done for real, Lamar, you'll see! So you might as well just head back to pack your shit and follow them back home because one of us have to go!"

"Man, fuck that, nobody is packing shit but the motherfuckas who are back there packing right now!"

Markus now immediately ask Chad to get Lamar just in time to overshadow whatever it is that Chris is about to say, because Chris says. "Look here," and Markus knew to intervene when he heard him say that because he interrupts him right along with Chad, who seems to know to intervene as well.

"Y'all know that they'll automatically send security or call the police if they hear y'all over that hill!"

Markus tries to be rational and says. "And I'm not trying to see no damn security or the police today, we didn't come way out here for this shit!"

"Chad, will you and Sky take me back to the cabin so that I can get my stuff? Apparently Lamar is staying, so I can just kill all of this right now and just leave."

"Yeah, we can take you."

Chad says when Lamar cuts in with. "I'll leave until you can think about this shit for a minute, but I'll be back because you know that I don't want that hoe!"

He now walks away to go and get back into the cart that he came in to completely shut down all arguments of who's doing what.

"Well, to make sure that it won't be another fight, I think that you ladies should probably just take a walk down by the water until we get back. We don't need for nothing else to jump off by having everybody back in the same place again. So Chad, you and Lamar can just take that cart, and I'll take this one back in case Yomme needs it for them to make a smoother transition. They probably won't need the carts, but both of them will be available to take them where they need to go. So ladies, we'll be back soon. Just stay down there by the water while I go and call the security house to have them to pull two trucks around." Chris instructs everybody, and we all follow his directions.

As he and Markus now take off in one cart, while Chad and Lamar takes off in the other. Leaving me, Sky, Rayci, and Kris to walk down by the water until they come back for us.

"I'm glad that he's calling to have them to bring the trucks around so that they can get the hell away from here." Rayci says. "But I think that Lamar really is going to try to come back for real after everything blows over."

"There's no such thing as blowing over in this situation, it'll never blow over in my eyes, so he don't even need to worry about coming back. I'm done with his bullshit for real this time, I mean I can't believe that he actually let this bitch put her mouth on his dick!"

"See, that's why I tried to snatch her damn head off!" Kris reiterates. "I knew that some foul shit was going on in that room!"

"I can't see how there has been two fights out here and I didn't know anything about neither one of them! I tried to help Nina with Tori because Chris had CJ, but I was so clueless to why they were fighting!" Rayci says, "But Markus told me what happened before we came to find y'all. He was like, Kris and Tori got to fighting in that back room, and then CJ and Tori got to fighting right after that. And I was looking at him like, where in the hell was I to have missed all of this? But then he started telling me how Lamar had told him and Chad that he had been drinking too much, and that he really didn't mean for any of this to happen. But Tori just wasn't taking no for an answer, because he said that he tried to stop her before Kris knocked on the door, but you don't believe him, CJ."

"I do believe that he may have tried to stop her after she had already started, but it just doesn't matter to me if he tried to stop her or not because it shouldn't have happened at all. But I guess everything does happen for a reason, so I'm not even going to sweat it because I'm done with him for real."

"Yep, everything does happen for a reason."

Rayci says. "But there's no reason why he should have been in that room with her, especially if he already knew that she liked him like that. Markus said that he set himself up for failure."

"Well, it worked because he failed, and I'm not even mad about it because I need to be solo until I can figure through my thoughts, anyway."

"That's true, but CJ, you still need to have fun like we came out here to do. Because they really didn't stop anything that wasn't about to be stopped anyway, if you really think about it."

Sky says. "So yeah, you should take this time out to figure through your thoughts and everything. But I feel like you still need to have some fun and enjoy yourself while you're here, treat this as a peaceful self-soothing vacation get-away."

"I know that's right!"

Rayci agrees with her. "A peaceful vacation mixed with a lot of fun because I'm ready to have some fun, too! We're just going to have to make sure that you still enjoy yourself while you're here because this isn't your fault!"

We all continue to walk and talk while also admiring how beautiful the wooded scenery is.

And we let almost an hour pass before turning around to head back to our original location, since we all decided to go ahead and walk a little farther past the water before going back.

In hopes of everything being taken care of by the time we make it back to the water.

CHAPTER 13
"LET'S GET IT STARTED"

W e finally arrive back at our original spot after enjoying our time away talking and sightseeing together.

And we only have to wait a couple of minutes before we see Markus coming for us with a cart.

"This is my second time coming down here looking for y'all, I waited down by the water for a long time before I drove around trying to find y'all!"

He says. "Chris and Chad are the only ones at the cabin now, everybody else is gone. Yomme and his people left in the truck they came in, and Lamar took ours, Ray."

"It's cool."

Rayci replies with relief. "Just as long as they're all gone!"

"And since it's a four-hour drive back home, he's just going to go and park the truck in our driveway when he wakes up in the morning, and I told him where to leave the keys."

"Good." She says. "Now we can go back to the cabin and start this trip all over again."

"Markus, what I want to know is how did y'all managed to keep Lamar and Yomme from getting into it out here? Yomme must really don't give a damn about her or what just happened out here!" Kris says because she still can't see how that argument was dodged.

"We told him that CJ and Tori were fighting over something that happened a little while back, so she's gotta leave. But I told him to call me or Chris when he gets back to the city so that we can rap."

"Aw, okay."

"But I'm going to tell him what really happened because that's my homie," Markus says. "Right now just wasn't the right time to tell him."

We all now get into the cart and go back to the cabin.

"See, look at this shit!"

Markus shouts at me jokingly, as we walk through the front door of the cabin and see the mess that was made before we left. "Now pick up this mess and then go to your damn room CJ, and don't come out until we tell you to!"

"That's fine with me because I'm going to my room after I pick this stuff up anyway. So thank you, and y'all won't have to tell me when to come out because I probably won't feel like coming back out here anyway."

And now while Sky and I clean up the mess, Kris and Rayci goes straight into the kitchen to make us some more drinks. Because Rayci is determined to have a do over by starting this trip with drinks, laughter, and fun memories.

"I need to go and get cleaned up before I start drinking anything for real. Because Sky, I've got so much on my brain right now that I might just get in the shower and then go to sleep. But then again, I might just come back out here and get stupid drunk."

"Yep, that's exactly what you should do." She says. "Forget that bullshit and let's party. Fuck it, let's get drunk!"

Now as we head into the kitchen, Markus soon comes in right behind us.

"Since you can't seem to make your way to your room." He says. "Let's blow some heads off one time, lil sis."

"Cool with me!"

I yell with excitement. "I'm about to go and take a shower to wash this pool water off of me, but you can still go ahead and break open that cigar box because I'm ready!"

"Okay."

He says. "I'll break it open and set you straight in a minute, and Chris said that he needs to holler at you ASAP. But now I think he just got in the shower, too."

And I'm glad to be standing right next to Kris while he says this to me. Therefore, if there are any problems with him wanting to come and see me when he gets out of the shower, this is her chance to voice her opinion on it without us having any confusion about it later.

"Good."

I reply, since she doesn't say anything. "Because I've got some shit to tell him, too, so you can just send him on into my room with that cigar box when he's done. I should be done showering and dressed by then. But if not, his ass will just have to wait until I'm dressed and ready for him to come in. Because I'm not about to rush, and it's not like I don't already know what he's about to say to me anyway. But I'm telling y'all right now that if he comes in there talking to me crazy, like I'm in trouble or something for fighting. Then I'll be taking that cigar box for myself, and throwing his ass out of my room for real."

And Kris is laughing with us and still hasn't said anything, or acted like she's upset or jealous about me wanting to talk to him or even about me asking that he be sent to my room when he's done. Yet for some reason, I still feel the need to ask her if she's okay with him coming into my room.

But unfortunately, the only thing about asking that question is that her answer would be irrelevant. Because if I know Chris, then he's still going to come in there and talk to me anyway. And tonight I need for him to do just that, so instead of me saying or even asking her anything. I'll just leave well enough alone and walk away, because if she's okay and quiet about it, then so will I be okay and quiet about it.

I now leave them to go and take a shower and to check to make sure that Lamar hasn't left anything behind.

Then I search through my things for something cute and sexy to lounge in after seeing that everything in my room is okay and in order. And although I know that it's wrong to pursue Chris when he comes in here, I don't care because he's honestly all that I've been thinking about since we've gotten back here.

And while it is weird to me because I feel like I should be thinking more about my breakup with Lamar instead. But I'm not, so I guess Chris will be getting exactly what he's been waiting for all this time.

So I go ahead and bring out my new vanilla, lavender, and jojoba oil body wash and lotion to try on and to reel him in with it. Then I begin to brush my teeth after putting on a shower cap and adjusting the shower water to the perfect temperature before getting in. But then I quickly snatch my shower cap off when I begin to lather my body and enjoy the ambience.

Because although it's only day one, I feel really good about my wavy hair being able to get wet every day and still look fabulous, just as my beautician promised.

And a shower is just what I needed because I'm starting to feel better already. And after I wash up and is about to get out—as soon as I turn off the water—I hear a knock on the bedroom door.

"Hold on, Chris!" I yell while grabbing my towel and running over to the door still wet.

I take a peek out to make sure that it's him. And it's him, standing and looking towards the living room area holding the big cigar box and a bottle of water. He's yelling down the hallway at everybody saying that he's only going to listen to me whine for a little while. And while laughing I also hear him saying. "Big brother my ass, tonight, I'm going to get her so high out here that she's not going to remember shit!"

"Shut the hell up and get in here, Chris!"

I order while clutching my bath towel to ensure that it doesn't fall off just yet.

I now rush back into the bathroom to finish drying myself off, but then I see him locking the bedroom door when I come back out.

So I walk over to the small speakers that my phone is plugged into, and I turn it down a little bit, only keeping it loud enough for us to enjoy the music and still be able to hear our surroundings. I immediately open the cigar box that he's placed on the table, and take out a tightly rolled blunt and light it.

"As you can see, I was just getting out of the shower when you knocked on the door. And I still have to put on some lotion and stuff so you're just going to have to overlook the fact that I'm not ready for you yet."

"It's all good, take your time and do it slowly."

He suggests as we both laugh.

"Don't worry, I will because I had to come over here and check out this cigar box first anyway. You know that I'm stressed out."

I now giggle while taking a few puffs from the blunt and then offer it to him.

"Here." I hand him the blunt. "Take this so that I can get dressed, and then maybe we can chitchat and clear up a few things."

"Nah." He says. "You need to go ahead and smoke that by yourself, Chase."

"Why?"

"Because if I hit it, then I'm going to get all horny and want to touch on you with you just standing here wrapped in a towel like this."

"That's cool because I'm over trying to stop you again if you try anything sexual with me, I'm ready for your ass now."

"Really?"

"Yep. Really, fuck it." I now place the burning end of the blunt into my mouth and hover over him to blow him a shotgun, whether he wants it or not.

And he wants it because his smile gets as wide as the room while he takes in the smoke. And it seems like my pussy can tell that she's about to be touched by how she's throbbing out of control already, just from being so close to him again.

And apparently his dick is doing the same thing because he pulls me down to sit on his lap after the shotgun is over.

And wasting no time at all, he all of a sudden picks me up and carries me over to the big arms chair that's sitting next to the window. But I lower my legs from around him to stand to my feet to say, "I don't want them to be able to hear us if we do this."

"They won't, baby."

He says. "But even if they do, Markus won't let nobody come knocking before he comes knocking first anyway."

And that's all I need to hear because I jump up to wrap my legs back around his waist again, as he grabs and smacks my ass while we kiss and caress each other.

I begin rolling my hips and pressing my body against his body, and he now turns around and lay me down on the big arms chair. And my body quivers tremulously when he begins to lunch on me like he hasn't eaten in days. His tongue is tackling my pussy like I'm going somewhere and he will never see me again.

"Damn, you taste good, CJ."

He mumbles. "Damn, you taste good."

And I'm thinking that it really has been a while since he's actually had some pussy for real, or maybe Kris's pussy just doesn't taste as good as mine.

Whatever the case may be, I'm enjoying it just as much as he is, so I'm just going to lay back and keep receiving his mouth while his tongue swiftly glides up and down my clit and in and out of everywhere.

But now he grabs my breasts when I open my legs more to give him as much as he wants, and it's a lot because he continues to suck and stick his tongue in and out of me while I moan and grab my own breast when he moves his hands and places them under me.

He's cuffing my ass while I relax my back and slightly lift myself up from the chair, while he's helping to hold me up and is feasting so well that I don't ever want him to stop.

But he have to stop when we eventually switch positions so that he can sit down in the chair, and I turn to the front with my back turned to him as I get on top of him and maneuver my pussy all the way up to his face, while his long overly grown cucumber-size dick stares me dead in my face like he's been waiting for me all day.

But I have to ignore how big he is so that I'm able to practice what I preach and just go for it, so I take a deep breath and slowly slide him into my mouth. While placing both of my hands on his legs, and I just let my mouth do all of the work while I continue to lick and suck on him as best as I can. And while I continue to suck and pop his dick in and out of my mouth, I eventually take him in as far as I can until I decide to slide down from his mouth and onto his dick. But I have to stop again and ask.

"Do you have any condoms?"

"Nope," he says. "Not on me, but we don't need a condom because I haven't been doing anything with anybody."

"Kris told me that y'all haven't been doing anything, but I think that we still need to use a condom."

"Come on, CJ, please don't do this right now. Lamar is always saying how you be making him wear a condom, so I know that you're clean. And I put this on my son and everything that I love when I tell you that I've been waiting because I don't want nobody but you."

"Well, let's just be careful because I guess we really have come too far to turn back now. Let's just pretend that there's one down there and keep going."

While laughing he agrees with me by grabbing me and kissing me like he's happy, and is about to show me just how much now that everything is a green light for us.

And since I've gotten up from our position, he stands up and places me right back on my back in the big arms chair, while he gets on top of me.

And as I'm trying my best to relax, while at the same time holding him tight as he sticks his rock hard dick in me and we begin to make love like it's our very first time ever doing it.

"We have to get in the bed."

He eventually moans in my ear while still stroking my pulsating pussy. Until we eventually transfer from the big arms chair to the bed, where I place myself on all fours while he gets in behind me doggy style.

But I quickly try to gesture for me to either lay back down on my back, or to just get on top of him. But it's too late because me being on all fours is already in motion, and there's no way that he's pulling out. So doggy style I receive, and doggy style I love.

And as we proceed, he eventually lay on his back so that I can get on top of him. And in my mind I'm thinking that I should just work him really good to get him off right quick, before someone comes knocking.

But my body is on a totally different page as our sex continues, because as I sit on his dick, I'm in delight city. Riding him like I have a point to prove, while at the same time pacing and adjusting myself because his dick is big.

And there's just no way that I'm about to rush him right now, especially not while he's cuffing my ass and squeezing on my breasts like he's doing. So I just roll my bottom in a circular motion while at the same time lifting myself up and down on him like I'm riding a bull in slow motion.

And he continues to accommodates me by holding my waist while our bodies become so attached that I'm willing to do just about anything to please him right now.

He begins to roll his hips as his dick goes deeper inside of me, and I don't resist him or his thrusts because he's right. Nobody can bring the pain like he can, so I grab onto the bed and just let my kitty do her thing now that she can see what she has to look forward to from now on. But within a matter of minutes, we both get a little too carried away with passion and start grinding and loving on each other so much that I know that we must ease up before he hurts me for real.

Because he has apparently forgotten that I haven't had his dick in a while, so I pull forward to lift myself up and only allow just his dick head to move in and out of me. But he pulls me closer to him and turns us over, and at this point he displays the very same behavior as he did the last time we did it, right before he popped.

He lifts my legs up as high as he can get them, and he tries to have his way with me because the sensual and tender strokes and loving thrusts have now stopped. And the fucking has begun because he's on ten and is ready to relieve himself, while I'm on full alert because I know that it's about to be a strong and powerful one. So I'm just enjoying letting him do his thing with his masculine strokes that are now stronger by the thrusts.

And the pressure is heavy because he cannot hold it in any longer because he releases everything that he can into me.

And he eventually rolls off of me with a smile on his face just as I have on mine because I feel free and on cloud nine.

"Okay, Chris, you're going to have to get up and go back out there so that I can get cleaned up. Then hopefully I'll be right out, too."

Seeming to ignore me, he doesn't say a word, so I wait for about a minute or so. And say, "Chris, you're going to have to get up and get out of here before it gets too late. Go and tell them that everything is OK with me and stuff."

And while looking up at the ceiling instead of at him, I still don't hear him respond to anything.

"Chris!" I yell while tapping him on his chest, as he now jumps up like his alarm clock has just woke him up.

"Hey!"

"'Hey!'" I repeat back to him, and ask. "Dude, were you sleep? Did you hear anything that I just said to you?"

We both laugh as he sits up so that he can make his way into the bathroom to wash up.

"My bad, baby, what did you say? I guess I dozed off just that quick, but now I'm ready to eat, take a shower, and lay down."

"First of all don't get used to calling me baby until after we can talk to Kris. Second, you cannot leave out of here to go and get back in the shower. And don't lay down, either, because Kris isn't stupid. If you go back in there wanting to eat and take another shower and lay down, she's going to know what just happened in here. And I don't feel like kicking her ass right now, so I think that you should just eat and then accidentally waste something on yourself in front of everybody before you get back in the shower."

"We'll see." He says like he can careless about what Kris or anybody else thinks, as he prepares to leave the room.

And only about three minutes after he actually leaves the room, I hear yet another knock at the door.

"Girl, let me in because I need to talk to you, open up! I just want to know if you're okay, now that you're probably in there high as fuck!"

Getting only a glimpse of my face as I open the door, Sky yells. "Dang, Smiley, weed don't make you smile like that! What were y'all in here doing—reading the Bible?"

She jokes with me while looking me over from head to toe like she's an inspector.

"What are you talking about, Sky?"

"I'm talking about you having a towel wrapped around you like you either just got out of the shower, or you're about to get in the shower. When if I'm not mistaken, you've been in here long enough to have showered before Chris came in here. So is this shower number one or shower number two?"

Chuckling, she continues as we walk over to the bed to sit down. "And what happened to your leg? Why are you walking like that?"

"Walking like what, there's nothing wrong with my leg."

"Whatever, CJ, y'all were probably in here doing something that you had no business doing anyway."

"No we weren't."

"I told you that y'all can't fool me, so how did you hurt your leg, for real?"

She asks again, as I'm laughing even harder now, but only amusing myself because I know that it's not my leg that's been hit and has me walking funny.

"I don't know what happened to my leg, but Chris and I was only in here smoking and talking. That's the only reason I'm smiling, I just needed a break from everything and everybody."

"Um-hmm." She mumbles with her lips pressed together like she still doesn't believe me.

"Anyway, I guess I'll just have to wait until you're ready to tell me the truth, because I know that something happened in here. So I'll just change the subject and let you know that Chad said that Lamar asked him to talk to you for him before he comes back out here tomorrow."

"Tomorrow? He told Chad that he's coming back out here tomorrow?"

"Yep, but Chad told him that he knows that he don't like to get into his personal business like that, but he told him that he should give you a little space to cool down before he tries to come back. Then maybe he'll have the chance to actually talk to you for himself, if he don't try to force his way back."

"Good," I sigh while shaking my head.

"I'm glad that he told him that because I do need some space."

"Yeah, you do. But I think it went into one ear and came out of the other one because he still ended up saying that he's coming back tomorrow. Because before they hung up, I heard Chad telling him that he don't want him coming back out here getting into any trouble. And y'all both know how Chad is, if it isn't about some money business for or with Lamar, then he pretty much stays to himself for the most part."

Sky now stretch across the bed while sniffing my lotion and putting some on her hands.

"You're right, he does stay to himself when it comes to things like this. But what do you honestly think that Chad will say or do when he finds out about me and Chris? Because him and Lamar may not be the best of friends, but they are real close, and they do a lot of business together."

"He's not going to say or do anything."

She says. "He wouldn't help you and he wouldn't help Lamar, because that's y'alls personal relationship. I think that he would

118

do his best to stay out of it unless it gets physically violent or something like that. Because one time he did ask me if you and Chris were creeping around, and I told him no. And when I asked him why did he ask me that question? He said that he was just curious, so I asked him what he thought Lamar would do if you and Chris were actually hooking up behind everybody's back for real. Literally just wondering, since the subject came up, not knowing that you two were actually doing the shit for real."

"Oh my God, for the last time we were not hooking up like that!" I yell while we both laugh, because I know that she does believe me at this point.

"Nah, I'm just playing. But for real, I asked him what he thought Lamar would do if y'all had been hooking up every day on the down low. And all he said was "nothing good", and those were his exact words. "Nothing Good". But I never thought to ask him what he would do because I pretty much know the answer to that question already. Just as long as he and I are on the same page, he doesn't care about who's doing who or what. So whether he finds out about y'all right now, or when we get back home, he'll probably just shake his head and listen to me talk about it whenever it comes up. But he definitely won't be doing anything like calling Lamar to tell him about it, and Lamar knows that Chad and Chris are friends with each other as well. So I'm sure that he knows that Chad wouldn't get involved in it either way."

Still rubbing her hands together, Sky now gets out of the bed and tells me that she's taking my lotion with her because it smells so good.

"I need to use it first, then you can borrow it."

I now walk away from her to go into the bathroom for a quick shower.

119

Then after I'm done showering, she's still in my room so I tell her. "One of my main concerns was Chad having to choose sides between Chris and Lamar. But I sure do feel a lot better now after talking to you about it, because I don't know what's about to happen out here Sky. I'm just glad that Lamar is gone for now, because I have a little more time to get things situated. So let's just get out of here and finish our conversation in the living room. Because I want to show my face so that everyone will see that I'm fine, and I actually don't have to be secluded to this room after all."

"Okay, that's cool. Go on and get dressed so that you can limp your handicapped butt on in there to the table so that we can play dominoes, instead of going to the living room. Because Kris and Rayci were in the living room before I came in here, and I know that you won't say much with Kris sitting there. So let's just go to the table."

"Okay." I agree, then get dressed to leave the room.

CHAPTER 14
"TREAD LIGHTLY"

I scan the room looking for Chris while Sky and I walk towards the dining room table, but I only see Chad, Kris, and Rayci. I don't see Chris or Markus anywhere.

"Rayci, where's Markus? I want to tell him about those pre rolled blunts that he sent in there that has me feeling super good and relaxed right now."

"Girl, he's in our room with Chris getting something, but he was trying to wait around to see the look on your face whenever you came out."

"He sure was, CJ."

Kris cuts into the conversation. "And Chris came out of there looking high as hell wanting to eat and lay down."

And right at this moment, it's taking everything in me to keep from laughing at her comment. Because he came straight out here and did exactly what I told him not to do.

"Well, I'm glad that you feel better, now all we have to do is get you liquored up! Then you'll really be over it!"

"I don't know, Rayci. I really don't think my body will let me take in any more liquor or anything else after smoking what I just smoked."

We all now take a seat at the dining room table as Rayci and Kris decides to join us, and that means that Sky and I will have to finish our conversation later. Because I really am not going to say much of anything with Kris sitting with us.

"We're about to play dominoes. What were y'all about to do?"

"Nothing much, so Kris and I can play with y'all if you want us to."

Rayci answers, and now asks Kris. "Are you down for some bones, Kris?"

"I might as well play since Chris keeps acting like I'm invisible and shit. It's like the more I want to talk to him, the more he ignores me. I really thought that he would be on something different after he smoked, but he's not. And if I don't say what's on my mind then I'm just going to burst wide open, because it's crazy to me how he'll smoke, drink, and kick it with you, CJ. But I can barely even get him to answer a simple-ass question for me anymore."

Instantly, and out of nowhere there's a vibe of her being friendly with me, while at the same time now letting me know that she does have an attitude about things.

So I ask. "What's that supposed to mean, Kris? I thought you were cool with him coming into my room to smoke with me. And if you weren't, then you should have said something to me or him before he even came in there."

"It's not just about him coming into your room because he was going to come in there whether I have a problem with it or not."

"Well, Kris, that's on y'all if he's going to do things anyway. Regardless of how you feel about it. That's something that you and him need to work on because it sounds like you still have a problem with our friendship. And you're just not flat-out telling me how you really feel about it, and I know that you don't hold your tongue for nobody. So what's up?"

"I'm just starting to feel like Chris is doing shit on purpose just to prove a point."

With her head down, she says. "I'm not even trying to start nothing with you, CJ, we've been there and done that a million times already. All I'm saying is that he can always seem to find time for everybody else but me, even out here, it's not just you."

And with her subdued tone, I look at Rayci and Sky in hopes of one of them saying something so that I won't have to say anything else, because this is just not the Kris that I'm used to dealing with.

So I'm just going to shut up because she has always been so straightforward and ready for an argument every time we have conversations like this. But now I guess I have to figure out how to deal with this new Kris, because the old one must really be gone.

And it's weird how much things have changed because now she actually does have a good reason to be snappy and ready to fight me.

Although I can't do anything about how Chris feels about her, because he's free to make his own decisions as a grown man. But I'm thinking that silence is going to be the best thing for me right now, because she needs some comforting. And I really don't think that I'm the one who should be comforting her, so I'm not about to say anything else until I'm asked a question or something.

Rayci now asks. "Are you still arguing with him every time y'all talk? Because that will make anybody shut down if they feel like they can't have a decent conversation with you without arguing all the time. And I'm only asking you that because I remember when you told me that you started an argument on purpose, just to get his attention one day."

"We don't even talk long enough for us to have an argument anymore. That's why I've been talking to everybody else about it—because he won't listen. And whenever we finally do talk longer than two minutes, it's only about little Chris, and I'm just so fucking sick of him acting like that towards me. I know that it was wrong to try to get his attention through an argument, but that's the only time that he would listen to me. But I don't even do that anymore because I've been trying to do things the right way, but he still treats me like I'm against him or something."

She now buries her face into her hands and inhales deeply, then she exhales deeper in frustration with her eyes closed.

"Well, I don't think that you should be holding your head down over this because what's meant to be will be."

Rayci says. "You can't force it, you just have to let things work themselves out by taking things one step at a time."

"That's what I've been trying to do, but I guess I need to come up with a different approach because I'm going to get his attention in one way or another. I'm sorry, Rayci, but with or without force he's going to listen to what I have to say before we leave this cabin."

"Well, I just hope that you think about your approach first before you go at him with any kind of special or unwanted behavior this time. You know that we're supposed to be out here having fun, not feeling stressed out and frustrated. So please just try to talk to him again calmly before trying some other approach, because any other way besides calmly won't get you very far with him anyway."

Rayci now suggests. "So let's just start this game so that we can all free our minds of any stresses that we may have. So who's going to keep score?" She now scrambles the dominoes together to mix them up so that we can start the game, while Markus and Chris now comes from the room laughing like they just heard or saw something funny.

And Chris still has the loving of me all over him because he still hasn't showered yet.

"I don't know why y'all are sitting at that table with those dominoes because none of y'all can play for real."

Markus says. "All you're going to do is make up your own rules then cheat on each other then get mad like there's some real money on the game."

"Right!" Chris says. "They won't be all happy like they are now in about twenty minutes, lil bro? Will they be smiling?"

"Hell nah!"

Markus shouts answering him as they both continue to tease us about how we are. "One of them is going to get an attitude, while the other ones quit. And then they're going to talk about each other and then start all over again like nothing ever happened, until one of them gets mad again."

"Whatever!" Sky says before telling them that they need to go and help Chad with all of that ice and beer that's on the deck.

"That's where we're headed anyway—to the deck. Come on Chris, and let me show you what I was talking about out here."

And as Markus and Chris begin to walk towards the entrance of the deck, Kris gets up and says. "Chris, I'm coming with y'all so that we can talk while we're out here."

She follows them out to the deck while we continue to start our domino game. Rayci says. "I feel kind of bad for Kris because I know that she really loves Chris, but it seems like it's too late to try to save their relationship now. It may have just run its course already because it sounds like she's fighting a downhill battle."

"Maybe so." Sky says while chuckling.

"And it's going to be an even bigger battle when she finds out that Chris has eyes for somebody else already."

"Who?" Rayci clamors in suspense. "Who are you talking about, Sky? I didn't know that Chris was seeing somebody else!"

I now place my forehead on top of my arms that are resting on the table so that I don't have to look at neither one of them, because things aren't going to be what they seem when she finds out that it's me.

"You really don't know who Chris is trying to get with, Rayci?" Sky continues to rant and chuckle while swaying from side to side like she's going to burst if she doesn't go ahead and let the secret out.

"I know that Markus has told you something!"

"Markus hasn't told me anything y'all, for real! I really don't know who he's trying to get with, I'm so lost for real!" Rayci says while hitting my arm as I look up while she's looking back and forth at me and Sky, and is seriously waiting for an answer.

Sky now grabs onto my arm and says. "Hold your damn head all the way up and claim your prize so that Rayci can solve this mystery right quick, Chase!"

She now starts gawking and pulling on me while looking at Rayci like I'm the one that they're talking about.

And now, promptly relieving me from having to answer whatever questions that Rayci is about to ask me, with her eyes and mouth bucked open like she can't believe it. Kris comes walking back inside from the deck and helps me to escape.

"Did you talk to him?" Rayci asks, while shaking her head as she redirects her attention from me to Kris.

But Kris sits down with us while still looking upset, and with no apparent plans of shaking things off, she answers. "Yeah, I talked to him, but he's still being ignorant so I said fuck it and just came back in here. I'm just going to leave it alone because all he's doing is pissing me off even more, but then when I snap on his ass, he's going to wish that he would've just talked to me."

"But what's going to happen when you snap on him other than him snapping back harder on you, Kris?" Rayci says. "I'm telling you what you should do for real, just wait until later because obviously he doesn't want to talk about it right now. But try to sit down and have a conversation with him later when it's just y'all, tell him that this is your last attempt at trying to get him to listen to you. Then just put everything out there, tell him that you want to stop stressing so that y'all can enjoy yourselves. And if he still don't want to listen, then move on without him and take in some Kris time and relax." Rayci urges her while standing to her feet just as I stand to mine.

"Where are y'all going?" Sky asks immediately, as if she doesn't want to be stuck at the table with Kris.

"You know where I'm going—into the kitchen for something else to drink." Rayci answers, then look at me. "Where are you going?"

"I'm headed to the kitchen, too. But not for anything to drink, so just sit right here and we'll be right back, y'all."

And as Rayci and I enter the kitchen by ourselves, she turns to me and says.

"I'm so for real about Markus not telling me about you and Chris! Girl, I didn't know that y'all were seeing each other like that! I guess I should have known that y'all had something going on, but a part of me just wouldn't believe it, and both of y'all have really been playing things off good because I really didn't know. But why didn't you tell me?"

"Because there was nothing to tell for real, Rayci. I mean we are going to try to be together now that he's told me how much he loves me and wants to be with me. But we haven't been creeping behind everybody's back this whole time or anything like that. We honestly just recently started having these deep sexually intimate feelings towards each other. And now we've decided to just go for it and see if things can work out romantically between us. Especially since he doesn't want to be with Kris anymore, and everybody already knows how Chris and I feel about each other. Apparently y'all can see it more than I thought because you're saying some of the exact same things that Sky was saying when I told her, but it really has been mostly innocent between me and him until now. Because things didn't truly start transpiring until we got out here to this cabin, and our feelings are mutual because I do know that I love him too. But I'll tell you more about what's happening between us later, because it's all just a big-ass headache for me right now."

"Okay, that's cool. Let's just be sure to talk about it later, because you know that I'm curious."

"Oh, we're going to chat about it because I want to explain to you how crazy this situation is."

"Okay."

She says as we pick up some wine and a few wine glasses to take back to the table with us, while she also grabs the bucket of ice that she just filled.

CHAPTER 15
"STOP TRIPPING"

Everything seems to be moving forward now that Kris has left the table once again, and Rayci gets up to go and check on Markus.

Leaving me and Sky alone again.

"Sky, I'm going to kick your ass for telling my business like that!" I bellow out while snatching a pretzel from the bowl that she's eating from.

"You may want to wait before you do that because I haven't said anything yet. I still have to tell Adrian and Indira about all of this drama that you have going on out here." She says while giggling like she's happy that they finally get to see me involved in some drama, instead of one of them.

And although I know that she won't tell them everything, I know that she's definitely going to spill just enough for them to have something to tease me about from time to time.

So I take the entire bowl of pretzels from her hands and get up from the table, but I immediately sit back down after I turn around and see Chris walking back inside from the deck.

And he walks straight over to us and asks. "What happened to the game? Y'all couldn't have cheated each other that quick."
"They knew that I was about to whip their asses, so they all backed out. That's what happened."
Sky answers him while laughing, then she takes back her bowl of pretzels.
I now stand up and back away from the table and whisper in a moderate volume. "Chris, why are you tripping with Kris like that? I mean really, she's not being mean or trying to fight nobody or anything like that, so why are you treating her like that for real?"
"I'm not doing anything to Kris, she's doing it to herself because I've already told her that I'm done talking about the same thing over and over. It is what it is, so she might as well get over it because I'm not about to let you, her, or anybody else make me talk to her when I've already said all that I'm going to say about our situation."
"Well, she's about to start acting up with you, and I don't want you to get mad and do something to her when all she wants to do is have a simple conversation with you! Your ass need to talk to her, and I don't give a damn that you've already spoke on it, maybe it is just what it is but that doesn't make it right! But I'm going to just stay out of it and let you handle it because you know that how you're treating her isn't right, and I'm not sure what you can do to make her understand! But I will tell you that it sure as hell isn't helping the situation out by you communicating with me and everybody else except her!"
"I feel you, but I've told Kris and everybody else who needs to know about me and her that I'm done with her and all of that. Like I said, I'm not going to keep repeating the same things over and over to her. And I'm done fighting with her anyway, regardless of what's going on between me and you, Kris knows what she's doing. This is beyond me and your relationship,

that's why I asked her not to come out here trying to start up some shit. I told you that I paid for everybody to stay here because she's not going to be happy until she makes herself mad enough to flip out. And now I guess she's going to take it upon herself to take things too far, but I don't care anymore."

I now shake my head and decide to leave it alone without trying to force him to talk to her, when he clearly isn't interested in conversing with her anymore at this point.

So I just walk away from the table to make my way over to the sofa to relax my body and my mind for a minute.

"Are you okay?"

Rayci comes over and asks, while taking a seat next to me as soon as I sit down on the sofa.

"Yeah, I'm okay. I've just got so much on my mind as far as Lamar and Chris are concerned, that I honestly am afraid that once everything is revealed to everyone. There really is going to be hell to pay, because I know that everyone is going to think that Chris and I have been sneaking around this whole time. But it really hasn't been going down like that, for real."

"Well, neither one of you are married, so technically you guys are free to do whatever you want to do. But you're right about what people are going to think because I have to admit, for a minute it did cross my mind that y'all didn't just end up feeling this way overnight like this. I thought that maybe y'all just decided to come on out with it now since Lamar did what he did."

She says while sitting back further on the sofa. "But if you say that y'all haven't been sneaking around, then I believe you. And I'm going to tell you just like I told Kris, don't be holding your head down about this situation because what's meant to be will be. Don't apologize or feel bad about who you love, especially nowadays, when true love is so hard to find."

"You are so right, Rayci."

"I know that I'm right, and I know that you feel me because you're always talking about when a person finds true love. They'd better hold on to it, so think back and remember that."

Then after a little while longer of sitting on the sofa and discussing life, we both eventually get up and start moving around again.

And things are slowly starting to improve throughout the cabin, because everybody seems to be enjoying themselves again for the most part.

Even Chris and I find ourselves exchanging comments and flirting now that we're all mingling. And Sky and Chad are still getting along, just as Rayci and Markus are.

Although I found out that Chris is paying Markus to hang around him instead of spending the majority of his time with Rayci. But Rayci is cool with it because she knows that if Chris is left alone with Kris, then things may not continue to go as well as they are now—so they're both just going with the flow of things. Although I do get tickled when Markus comes to tell me about his terms of agreeing to hang around Chris right now, because he says that this trip is supposed to be for him and his wife to get in some fun times together without their kids.

Not for them to come out here and play keep away with us.

"While Kris is in there changing clothes, y'all need to be figuring out how you're going to get rid of her ass for real." Markus says. "Because Ray and I are going to hang out with y'all for a little while longer, but we can't block for you all night. Eventually we're going to have to separate before we go to bed."

"That's what we're about to do right now, let's figure out what's about to happen and how. Because we need to also figure out what we're going to do about Lamar if he comes back out here."

"CJ, nobody is worried about Lamar. And as far as Kris goes, if y'all want me to, I'll just tell her that they just faxed over an eviction notice with just her name on it, so she's gotta go." Markus says while smiling. "For real, she can just take the last truck and leave, or she can just fly back home or something. I'm sure we can figure it out some kind of way."

Chris and I laugh at him because he's joking, but it would actually be a good idea if something like that could happen for real.

But sending her away in the last truck left, or even taking her to the airport so that she can catch a flight back home is just not going to happen for real.

"I'm not going to sit here and draw out some sort of strategy that we should use on her or Lamar, we're just going to let this shit happen however it's going to happen."

Chris says. "For real, they'll have to accept it and move on."

"I understand that you don't want to come up with a plan, but I have to because Lamar will be coming at me tomorrow not you."

I continue with a bit of frustration.

"And I know that you or Markus won't let him come at me wrong, but I just don't want to see this all blow up out here when we can simply just come up with a plan on how to handle this right now."

"It's not going to blow up, baby, things won't be as bad as you think."

"I sure hope not, Chris, because I don't want you to get upset when I know that Lamar is already going to be upset when he finds out that we're truly over. Because then what's going to happen if you both end up getting upset and stop listening to any reasoning from anybody, including me?"

"Like I said, it's not going to get like that because they both are just going to have to accept it and move on. And I'm not going to get mad because I know that it's kind of wild how things are turning out, so I already know what to expect and what to avoid.

Now in the meantime, I want to know if we can still get together later to finish our conversation from earlier, and I want some more kisses and stuff too."

"See, Markus, listen to him!"

Now directing my attention to Markus instead of Chris.

"I guess I should be having this conversation with you right now because your brother seems to be disregarding everything that's being said to him by talking about us hooking up even more right now!"

Markus laugh with us while Chris says. "I know that we have to be careful."

"We have to be more than careful and just wait until after everything calms down before we have any more one-on-one time. I mean really, Chris, how are you going to ask to meet up again when Kris will probably be on you all night trying to get you to communicate with her? And in all honesty, we've probably done enough talking for today anyway. I'm just now starting to walk straight from after our last 'talk', so I don't think that we should do any more 'talking' until tomorrow."

Giggling while still trying to be serious, I look at him and try my best to stop smiling to show him that I'm so for real about not meeting up with him anymore tonight.

And before either of us can say anything else, Kris comes walking from their bedroom and makes her way over to us.

But I take it upon myself to lie and tell them that I will be right back, after I go and get myself some water—but I walk away from them with no intentions of coming back. Because I'd rather just be with myself and walk away, rather than to hang around and be fake with Kris right now.

CHAPTER 16
"PLAY RIGHT"

Markus is grabbing and kissing all over Rayci—and they are clearly enjoying each other's company—but with his obligations to help Chris. Markus stops and asks everybody if we want to play truth or dare.

"We're too old to be playing truth or dare." Rayci says. "I get onto the kids for playing that game sometimes because you actually have to tell the truth or do your dare for real if you're going to play it right."

"I don't want to play because these dudes will be daring us to do some crazy off-the-wall-type of stuff, and you know the questions will be even worse."

"What's the matter, Chase? Are you scared that we're going to dare you to do something strange for a piece of change?" Chris says while amusing everyone as we all come together like it isn't up for debate whether we're playing or not. Because we all participate by taking a seat, while I do my best to try not to complain about how bad of an idea I think this game is for us right now.

135

And with Chad being just as eager to play as everyone else, he starts the game off by daring Rayci to take three shots of tequila in a row within ten seconds.

Because he knows that Rayci feels like she must have all of her drinks mixed with something, so he dares her to drink the strongest tequila that he can find without letting her mix it, or chase it with anything. Or she could've chosen to tell the truth about whatever he wanted to ask her, but she chose the dare.

Now after Rayci and Chad have their turn, we all agree that it should be Markus's turn to take a truth or dare.

And then after him, it's me and Sky's turn, and Sky doesn't hesitate when it's our turn to go.

She says. "Okay, CJ, truth or dare?"

"Truth."

"Okay, out of everybody in this room, who do you love the most and why?"

She asks while looking at me smiling, as if she already know that I'm about to say her name. But I yell. "Chris, and not Sky!" I laugh while shaking my head at her. "Burst your bubble, didn't I? I mean what kind of question is that for you to ask me when you know that I love everybody in this room all the same. And the reason I said Chris's name is because I've known him the longest out of everyone else in this room, so you should have picked another question because that one was slanted."

Chad yells. "That wasn't slanted, it was whack! And if we're going to play then we have to get down and dirty with it, or the game is going to be boring!" He now volunteers to go again, "Truth or Dare, Chris?" He says while scratching his head like he's really trying to think of a good truth or dare for him.

Chris replies. "Truth."

"Damn, man! I was hoping that you would say dare, but I guess my dares are a little too far out there for you after seeing Rayci taking those shots, huh!"

"Hell nah! I just chose truth because that was the first thing that popped in my head when you asked me."

"Man, I was getting a dare ready for you in my head—that's why I said your name—but I can't seem to come up with a good question for you right now."

So Chad takes the easy way out and says. "If you were stuck on a deserted island, and only one of us from this room could be with you, which one of us would it be and why?"

Laughing and frowning at the same time, Chad tells us that he's just going to be like Sky and ask this bullshit ass question. Because he can't think of a good question for real, and he tells us that he likes it better when people choose dare.

Chris says. "I'll go on and answer this question truthfully, and then my next turn will definitely be a dare. Because I don't want to play either if we're going to be tiptoeing around the game. And Chad, don't be trying to back out when I dare your ass to do some crazy-shit!"

"Bet!"

Chad agrees with him excitedly, like we're about to make the game raw and uncut for real this time.

"So to answer his question, I would pick Chase to be stuck on a deserted island with me."

He says while reaching down to grab his drink like it's okay for him to say my name, when he could've easily said Markus or Kris's name, since they're both sitting right here too.

"Chase!"

Kris gets up and scream. "Why in the hell would you choose Chase?"

"Because if I had to choose somebody from this room to be stuck on a deserted island with, I would choose Chase."

He continues while still acting like he hasn't said anything wrong. "This is truth or dare, right? I'm choosing to tell the truth, unless y'all want me to lie about it!"

And I just sit and listen to them in silence, feeling shocked that he said my name, but I'm ready for her to say something to me next.

"What the fuck am I missing for you to sit up here and say that you would want to be stuck on an island with CJ instead of me? What the fuck is really up, Chris?"

She screams while looking mad enough to kill him with her eyes.

"I'm not trying to be disrespectful, Kris. I just answered the question truthfully, so let that shit go and let's just move on with this game."

"I'm so for real right now, I'm going to need for you to stop treating me any kind of way like I don't mean shit to you!"

She yells at him, then finally looks over at me, and with a slight attitude she asks. "CJ, what's up? Am I missing something here?"

"I don't know if you're missing something or not, I can't help it if he wants me on the island with him!"

"Kris, I need to talk to you for a minute."

Chris steps back in, now getting up and gesturing for her to follow him into their room.

"Let's go to the bedroom for a minute, we can finish this game later."

She stands still for a few more seconds, and then she follows him while giving me a look of suspicious backstabbing hatred.

And even though she has every reason to be looking at me like this, I look right back at her in the same manner as if she's done something to me.

But now after she and Chris goes into their room, Markus says. "CJ, she was about to beat your ass!"

Laughing while throwing his hand towel across his shoulder, he says. "I was sitting here thinking about what I was going to do to help you if she would've just popped you in your face, sis!"

"Never will any Bitch just pop me in my face and not get dealt with! And I wouldn't have needed your help because I can handle this shit myself!"

I yell back at him in a serious but still in a jokingly manner. "So if she was thinking about doing some shit like that, then you see that she quickly thought twice about it, and chose otherwise!"

"I knew that she wasn't going to hit you because she don't know what's really going on for real."

Markus says. "All he said was that he would choose to be on a deserted island with you, but there's no telling what he's in there saying to her right now though."

"You should go in there and tell him not to tell her right now."

Rayci says. "I think that he should just wait because she's going to be so hurt."

"Look, everybody is going to find out sooner or later anyway."

Chad nonchalantly comment, while Sky and I look at each other in suspense, not knowing that he knew anything about me and Chris liking each other in a romantic way.

He says. "Whether he wants to tell her right now, or if he wants to wait until later—either way it goes. Somebody will probably end up getting fucked up behind all of this shit anyway."

"How do you know about what's going on, Chad?"

Sky says. "You haven't said anything to me about them."

"Chris told me what was going on while y'all were waiting for us down by the water earlier. But I didn't think that he would say no shit like that in front of her right now, but he got it. I told him that I don't get into his personal business or Lamar's, and they don't get into mine so whatever they all have going on is between them. We're all good because I don't have anything to do with it at this point either way."

"I think that Kris is trying to save something that just can't be saved." Sky says as she stands up to stretch.

"But like my man says, that's between them, so I'm going to leave it alone and just hope for the best. Because they're all crazy if you ask me—even you, CJ, while you're over there sitting on deserted islands and shit!"

Loving her sense of humor, we all laugh.

"Well, that tequila has me feeling a little woozy right now is all that I have to say." Rayci intervenes while getting up and waving her hands back and forth in front of her face like she's trying to take in some extra air.

She says. "I'm over here sweating and everything, I think I need to go and get me some water or something!"

"Okay, Rayci, go and get your water. Then come on back so that we can finish this game because the party is just getting started." Chad says again, as if Chris's truth wasn't enough to ruin the game.

And as we're about to start the game again, Chris comes from the bedroom and asks me if I will come in there with him and Kris for a minute.

But I look at him with a don't-fuck-with-me type of expression on my face, because I know that he can't possibly think that we're going to be able to solve this by sitting down and talking things out like mature adults.

"What exactly are you trying to do here, Chris? Because you couldn't have told her anything if you're out here asking me to come in there with y'all. And I know that we've had our ups and downs, but I'm not even trying to hurt Kris like this. It's not even about who can fight the best or who will end up being with you because I know how you feel. But it seems like I care more about her feelings than you do, so I'm not going in there to talk to her right now."

I now cross my legs to get more comfortable in my seat, as if I'm not about to get up and go anywhere.

"Did you tell her?" Rayci inquires while still fanning herself like she's hot.

"Nah, I just talked to her again about us and our relationship right quick. And I told her that I have something else that I want to talk to her and CJ about together, because I don't want her to know that CJ already knows how I really feel about her. So I'm about to just break the news to both of y'all at the same time, so just act surprised or whatever, CJ."

He now comes closer to me and says. "This will help to ease things between y'all so will you just act like you don't know anything about what I'm about to say? I'm only asking that you do this to show her that this isn't your fault, and that you are just as surprised as she will be to hear what I have to say."

"I cannot believe that you're about to do this right now!" Sky says as the truth-or-dare game officially comes to a halt. "What is she in there doing?"

"She's in there wiping her face and getting herself together while I come to get CJ, because I told her that I only want the three of us in the room."

He now redirects his attention back to me and says. "And if we do things the way I'm asking, then if things do get out of control, it will be with me and her instead of you and her."

"I'll come in there with y'all, Chris. But like you told me for when it's time for us to deal with Lamar. I'm going to handle my business regardless of what you say if she comes at me wrong, you're out of it. Because I'm telling you right now that things are going to get out of control when she finds out, and although I don't want to fight her because I understand her pain. But I'm still not backing down from Kris."

I reassure him while uncrossing my legs to stand up. "And I'm going to tell you this, too. I'm not about to be arguing and fighting with Kris all the time about this. I don't mind whipping her ass once or twice, but that shit is going to get old real fast.

141

Because I promise you that you and I will end up remaining strictly friends before I allow myself to deal with this foolishness on a regular basis."

"It won't even be like that, Chase. Just follow my lead and everything will be fine."

And Kris is now about to come from the room right as we approach the door to open it.

"I had to convince her to come in here because like you, she thinks that something weird is going on, Kris."

Chris says to her while the three of us now go into their room. "Let's just come on in here so that I can clear up all of this suspicion and tell both of you how I'm feeling."

And now my only thoughts are to make sure that I don't get out of my element before she does.

So I'm just going to stay as quiet as I can while he breaks this news to her and see what happens. Because I understand that he's trying to preserve anything that can be preserved between me and Kris.

But there is nothing that he can do to save our relationship because she loves him way too much to forgive us or accept us as a romantic couple under any circumstances.

CHAPTER 17
"I HATE YOU"

I walk over to sit in the big arms chair by the window that looks just like the big arms chair in my room that Chris and I had sex on earlier.

I sit patiently while fondling my bracelet and waiting for Chris to say something else, while Kris stands against the wall staring at me.

"First of all, Kris. Chase don't know what I'm about to tell you just like you don't know what I'm about to say. But this shit has to be said out loud and in the open and in front of both of you, and I think that this is the best time for me to say it because I can't hold it in no more. And hopefully neither one of you will get too mad at me over this, but what can I say? I've tried to fight it, but I can't help the way I feel."

He now walks away from the door entrance after closing the door all the way and continuing to talk.

He asks Kris. "Why didn't you answer me earlier when I asked you why did you come on this trip when I asked you not to come?"

"I came because I wanted to spend some time with you, because every time I talk about us going on the cruise to try to fix things, you blow me off! And I knew that this would probably be our last getaway together, since you're trying your best to remove me and your son from your life!"

She screams at him while moving closer to him like she's ready for whatever.

"Little Chris don't have shit to do with this, so stop bringing him into our shit every time we argue!"

He yells back at her while she now stands directly in front of him.

"So you're just on to the next one, huh, Chris? I guess I should be happy that you have at least narrowed us down to relationships now, instead of a different bitch by the hour! Who's after CJ? Sky?"

She wails with a disappointed look on her face, as if she already knows what he's about to tell us before he even say it.

"I guess Sky will be after you, Chase!"

She continues to talk louder and louder after each word, while she's now talking to me but still looking at Chris.

"You know that I'm not on to no motherfucking next one!"

He roars back at her. "I just have to let you know that if I'm going to settle down and be with just one woman for the rest of my life, I want to be honest about it and tell you that I can't see myself making that kind of commitment with nobody but CJ! And I really didn't want to tell you that out here like this, but you just won't listen to me when I tell you to move on and get with somebody who will love you like you should be loved! And you know that I'm not even trying to be rude and shit, but I feel like I have to be rude to you and throw something in your face or be an asshole for you to really hear me!"

Kris now look past him and at me with tears in her eyes, but she doesn't say anything to me.

144

She quickly places her attention back onto him, and with plenty of rage, hatred, and animosity in her voice, she shouts.

"You sneaky motherfuckers!"

"I tried to tell you to stay your ass at home and let me come out here by myself so that I can figure this shit out first, but you had to make your way on out here anyway, like you can stop some shit that's out of your control from happening! I damn near begged you to stay at home so that I can figure this out, because I didn't know how I was going to tell you or CJ!"

"Nah, you wanted me to stay at home so that you and CJ could come out here and have your way with each other! That's what you wanted to do!"

"He couldn't have planned to come out here and have his way with me because I came out here with Lamar!"

"Whatever, CJ!"

But she now says to Chris. "No wonder you're always putting her up on a damn pedestal about something all the time, nobody's that damn close!"

She continues to shout while now trying to get around Chris to get closer to me like she doesn't believe that I came out here to only be with Lamar.

"You can let her go or get past you or whatever it is that she's trying to do Chris, because even though I didn't know that you felt this way until now! She's going to think whatever she wants to think anyway!"

I continue to shout. "But Kris, if you break free after doing all of that pushing and pulling, I'm going to beat your ass because I know how you are! And I know that you're mad but I'm just as surprised as you are!"

"Neither one of y'all will be fighting out here because I didn't call y'all in here for this bull-shit!" Chris shouts while continuing to hold on to Kris as she tries harder to get around him to get to me.

But I do just as he asked me to do, I'm standing still in one spot and waiting for her to make her way over to me, instead of getting mad and making things worse by approaching her. Because although I am saying bad things to her, in all honesty, I don't blame her for being mad. I would probably be mad, too. But she needs to realize that I'm not the one who broke her heart—he is.

But she's already mad at me so I know that she's not going to rest until we have a brawl, and I know that I'm going to have to give her what she want.

"I said let her get by you so that we can go ahead and get this one out of the way, Chris! Because it's going to have to happen sooner or later anyway!"

"Bitch, that's so fucked up for you to be fucking him behind my back when I trusted you, hoe!"

She now fights even harder to get closer to me.

"You can stop all of that shoving like you're really about to go hard when I'm trying to tell your ass that I haven't been fucking him behind your back! I'm just as surprised as you are about this shit, Kris! I didn't know that he liked me like that until now!"

I shout while watching her push and push until she gets close enough to grab her cell phone from the bed to throw at me.

And when I turn my head she barely misses my lips when she throws it at me so hard that it hits the wall and breaks into three pieces. I now immediately run straight towards them and there is nothing that Chris can do about it at this point.

"Kris!"

Chris shouts. "Chase! Stop!"

He now wrestles with the both of us while trying to keep us apart, but I've already snatched her from his arms so fast and started punching her in her face as hard as I can. While she reaches up and grabs a big chunk of my hair and starts hitting me also, but I quickly pull away from her so that she can't hit me. But she has my hair so I swing and pop her directly in her jaw, forcing her to let me go. Right as I see her fist coming towards my head, and I feel it when it lands sharply against my ear.

But now after hitting her in her eye a few times, I know that she can feel the impact because she keeps trying to lean on me and Chris.

But I push away from her so that she can't grab me again, because I'm not about to let her get me on the floor or the bed, she'll have to kill me first. — Because I for damn sure am trying to hurt her in any way possible right now.

Suddenly, I feel a really tight grip on my arm, followed by a horrible sting.

So I use the weight of her body and my strength to get her by the table and to slam her face onto the table, while at the same time still punching and hitting her and Chris.

But now everybody comes running into the room to help break us up.

"Man, we saw this shit coming from a mile away, Chris!" Markus shouts while helping him and everybody else to break us up.

"I knew that it was about to be a fight before you even closed that door! But damn, look at all of this blood, it looks like y'all was having a dogfight in here! Acting like some fucking pit bulls fighting over my brother like this!"

Markus yells. "I mean look at this shit!"

"Bitch, this shit ain't over, just wait motherfucka!"

Kris shout at me while still trying to break free from Markus, as I stand partially in front of her while being picked up and carried out of the room once again by Chris from yet another fight.

147

"Right, it's not over Bloody Mary!" I shout. "Get on before you get popped again, bitch! While you're over there acting like you're really trying to break free!"

I continue to snap at her as Chris gets halfway through the door with me.

"I see what's up with you, you backstabbing bitch! That's why I tried to bite your fucking arm off, slut!"

But Chris carries me out of the room and close the door so that I won't hear anything else that she's saying, although I don't want to hear anything else from her anyway.

Nor do I want to look at her bloody and soon-to-be-swollen face anymore. But as I look down at my arm, right next to my elbow there's a bite mark that's shaped like a human's mouth because she literally just tried to take a chunk of meat from my arm.

"I bet that bitch is going to have a migraine headache while she's in there trying to keep from going blind in one eye! And Chris, you know that I'm not for all of this fighting and shit, while you're calling me in there with y'all in the first place! So don't be looking at me like that because this is your fault, and I'm pissed off because I told you that this would happen!"

"Why didn't you just sit down when I asked you to? Maybe we could have avoided this!"

"Shut up Chris! I know that you didn't just say that this could've been avoided, because you and I are about to have a big problem in a minute because you got me fucked up! And I'm about to say fuck you too because you're not this damn off track with shit, I'm not about to just stand still when she just threw a fucking phone at me that barely missed my lips! And I didn't volunteer to come in there to fight or go back and forth with her, now you're telling me that all of this could have been avoided? Really, Chris, fuck you!"

I now give him a look that's pretty similar to the look that Kris gave him after he told her his true feelings for me.

"All I'm saying is that y'all didn't have to fight like that—that's all—especially when it's concerning me because you know where my heart is! I wanted you to ignore her, but I'm sorry because it is my fault for taking you in there without thinking the whole thing through first."

He apologizes as he now comes closer to me to look at my arm. "I didn't think that she would throw anything at you, I just knew that I wasn't going to let her get close enough to touch you. And I definitely didn't think about you coming for her like you did, but now I see that it was a bad idea. But I really did think that we could talk things out since I was being honest with y'all."

"I'm sorry for popping off, but you know that I don't fight over no man, not even you. I'm too cute for all of that, but I was not about to let her get away with throwing that phone at me like that. Thankfully I turned my head so it hit the wall, but I also knew that we weren't going to be able to talk things out without a fist fight first, because I know that she feels betrayed."

"What all happened in there? All of a sudden we heard stuff falling and banging and slamming! Man, we just knew that all hell had broken loose when we heard Chris shouting and cursing! And I almost broke my damn leg trying to get through that door to see what was going on!"

Sky laughs as she comes and join our conversation. While also informing us of what they were all saying and doing now that the truth is out.

"Right now, Chad and Rayci are in there doctoring and trying to calm Kris down. Because she's saying that it's messed up how Chris is out here checking on you, CJ. Instead of her, when she's the mother of his child. She said that she just can't believe that y'all would do this to her like this in her face."

"I tried to tell her that it's not like that, but she don't want to hear that shit at all! I mean I don't blame her for not believing us, but I knew that this fight had to happen!"

I now continue to shake my head at the thought of us maybe having to fight every time I see her.

"I told her that it's a messed-up situation, but y'all should probably try to sit down and talk things out before y'all leave here. But as you can imagine, she wasn't interested in hearing anything that I had to say, so I just left and came out here."

Sky continues, until she looks down at my arm. "Girl, look at your arm, y'all had to have been in there rumbling because her face and head is fucked up, and she's pissed!"

Markus now comes walking up on us. "There have been three fights out here that I've had to break up, and you and Kris have been in just about all of them!"

"That's more fights than I've seen all month!"

Chad says while taking a seat at the table after he has left Rayci in the room with Kris.

"Chad, you left Rayci in there by herself?"

Sky asks while laughing, knowing that Rayci probably don't want to be left in there by herself right now.

"I had to come out because Kris is on some other stuff. She's listening to Rayci a little bit, but I think the only other person who's going to be able to calm her down is Chris."

"Maybe you should go in there and check on her, Chris."

I suggest while still trying to push some sort of good after all of this.

"I'm checking on who I need to be checking on, so stop trying to force me into talking to her when you don't know what I've been going through with her. I'm done with all of that, she'll have y'all thinking that she just needs to talk to me. But trust me—she'll be fine."

He now tells Markus. "Go back in there and check on her for me lil bro, and tell her that she's gotta stop it."

"I'll go in there and check on her for you, but you know that she's not going to listen to me."

Markus says. "Chase, you should go in there and ask her to calm down in your nice voice. Then maybe she'll start listening to you, just go and hug her then say something nice."
"Ha, ha, ha."
I respond with a fake laugh.
"You need to go in there and help your wife."
"I hope that you can talk some sense into her because she sure as hell wasn't listening to me!"
Chad says in a somewhat bothered tone.
"She almost called me out of my name, so I just came on out of there! She was like, fuck you too Chad!"
We all now laugh because we can actually picture Chad walking straight out of there without a hesitation after she started talking to him like that.

CHAPTER 18
"LOVE HURTS"

Somehow Kris must have convinced Markus to come and ask Chris to come back into their room so that they can talk, because he comes over and tells Chris that he needs to talk to him.

And I can clearly see that he wants to talk to him in private by how he's whispering something really low so that I can't hear him.

"You can go on over there and talk to him, Chris, because I don't want to hear about anything that she's plotted anyway."

"Be quiet, CJ, and go somewhere and get a tetanus shot or something."

Markus continues to joke around with me while he and Chris walk away from me.

"Chase, if things are like this between you and Kris now, I can only imagine how things will be if you and Chris start hooking up on a daily bases."

"I know right, fighting every day. But I will never be in that type of relationship, never!"

"I feel you, because it's a mess, and Rayci is the only person that she will even come close to listening to." Sky says as we sit and nurse on my arm.

Now Markus walks towards the kitchen area while Chris surprisingly walks back into their room with Kris and Rayci.

And a few minutes later, Markus comes over to sit with us after getting himself a cold beer to drink.

"Chase, if you get into another fight out here. I'm going to personally beat your ass myself, I promise."

"Don't come over here messing with me right now!"

Rayci now comes from the room before I can finish feuding with him, and she has a look of relief on her face as she comes and sit down beside Markus.

"Girl, what's going on in there?" Sky asks.

"Kris is in there tripping."

Rayci says. "She was trying to come out here and see what Chris was doing, until Markus came and asked him to come back in there and talk to her. And I knew that I couldn't let her come out here so that she and CJ could fight again. But CJ, for a minute I felt like saying. "Go ahead, Kris," because I was not about to keep fighting with her about not coming out here! Lord knows I was happy to see Chris come through that door right before I was about to give up!"

"I told him that he had to take his ass in there because she's acting like she's about to lose her mind or something."

Markus says. "And when I told him what she was in there saying about him and CJ, he almost blew a fuse. But I told him not to go in there blowing up on her, but he did need to go in there and check her ass one good time because when Kris starts talking like that, he knows that she'll do that shit for real."

"What is she in there talking about doing?" I ask while becoming more alarmed with thoughts of her trying to do something crazy to me or my family.

"Don't you worry about what she's in there talking about doing, because you've done enough damage as it is, so just be seen and not heard; OK?"

We all burst into laughter again at Markus's sense of humor.

"Shut the hell up! I just know that she'd better not be in there talking about doing something crazy to me or my family!"

And we all just continue to talk and go back and forth about what's happening, and then Rayci tells me that Kris told her that she had an idea that Chris liked me more than he was admitting. But she said that she really didn't think that we would be going behind her back like this, and right as Rayci is talking. We hear what they had obviously heard coming from Chris and Kris's room earlier when we were in there fighting.

Because we all jump up to go running to see what is going on for us to be hearing all of the loud crashing sounds mixed with clumsy furniture moving like someone is fighting.

"Yo! Wait a minute!" Markus yells while running over to grab Chris.

"I told you if you ever tried some shit like that again, I would make your ass disappear! Let's grab yo shit and bust a move bitch!" Chris shouts while one of his hands is around Kris's neck, while holding her against the wall with her feet no longer touching the floor.

But Markus grabs him with all of his might to keep him from doing even more damage to her.

"I want you to hurt me, motherfucker, that's what you like to do anyway!"

Kris cries out. "Go ahead and hurt me, kill me!"

She now gets a glimpse of me looking at her flipping out, and she says. "Bitch, what the fuck are you looking at with your shady ass? I should have known that y'all was fucking around when he stopped fucking me to come and hang out with your two-faced ass!"

154

"You're looking real stupid out here clowning trying to fight everybody, Kris, I told your ass that we haven't been doing anything! But I'm going to just get out of here because you're not trying to hear shit anyway!"

I now turn around and walk out of the room.

Chris can do whatever he wants to do with her, but I know that I need to just stay out of sight.

So I leave their room and head towards the sofa to have a seat, but I'm just now realizing that I still haven't taken in that me time that I really do need right now to get away from absolutely everything and everyone for real.

So I change directions and head to my bedroom instead of relaxing on the sofa, I can wait and talk to everyone bright and early in the morning because I truly am done for tonight.

CHAPTER 19
"BRAINPOWER"

Feeling serene and at peace for a moment back in my room alone, I feel like my healing process can begin.

But as soon as I gather my thoughts, I'm starting to notice that my room may not be as peaceful as I would like it to be because every time I close the door, it seems like somebody comes to knock on it ten minutes later.

I've only had time to wash my hands and face when I hear the knocking on the door.

"Chris, why are you trying to come in here after everything that just happened? Damn, are you trying to make that girl lose her mind? Because I'm starting to think that you are doing this shit to her on purpose, because it's one thing to confess your love for me! But now it seems like you're trying to torture her by coming in here, and I'm not about to help you do that shit, so you need to leave me the hell alone before I get mad for real! I'll talk to you tomorrow, bye!"

I now step back so that I can close the door.

"Come on, Chase. Let me in, I wouldn't be knocking at your door if she was out here watching. She don't know where I am right now, I just need to talk to you because I don't like what you just saw between me and her. That's why I wanted to keep my distance from her, because when I try to explain something or straighten things out with her on how I feel about anything. If she's mad then she won't allow me or anyone else to be civilized with her, and she knows exactly what to do and what to say to make me want to hurt her."

I now move out of the door entrance to let him come inside after looking down the hallway myself to see who can see him coming in, but I don't see anybody.

"Rayci and Markus are talking to her for me because she finally calmed her ass down and started listening to somebody for a change."

He continues while walking over to sit on the bed while stressing to me how hard he tried not to put his hands on her.

"I'm taking her ass home tomorrow, unless she starts tripping again and force me to call Chauncey to come out here and get her ass tonight."

"She's not going to give us any peace as a couple, and I don't have time to be dealing with Kris like that all the time. And you see how she threw little Chris's name into the mix already. You know that if we go forward with this, she'll make both of your lives a living hell because of me."

"That's why I've already told my lawyer that we're going to have our hands full when it's time to deal with her as far as me seeing my son, so he advised me two months ago to go ahead and remove anything personal from the house that she could use against me, and I did. Even though she's never had access to anything that's really important anyway, but when the courts get involved, I want to be sure that my shit is set straight and waiting for whatever bullshit that she may have. Although we're not married, so I always limited what I would tell or show her anyway. But Kris knows how far is too far when it comes to dealing with our son."

"Out of all the women that you were with, you had to settle down and get the craziest one pregnant!"

I now sit down while shaking my head, as he shakes his head also.

"She didn't start acting like that until after she got pregnant, because we were happy before the pregnancy. She had a few kinks that needed to be worked out, but so did I, so we just made it work. I even thought that I could be with her one day as her husband, but that thought came and left the same day and never came back."

"She had some things, but I don't know if I would call them only a few kinks. That's putting it nicely Chris. But she can be a good person at times, especially lately, so I understand what you're saying. I just feel bad because this situation really isn't her fault, but it just is what it is."

"Right, but I didn't come in here to discuss my relationship with Kris with you. I just really want you to know that I do think about you a lot every day, and I know that we both will be jeopardizing a lot to be together. But I promise you that it's not going to be as bad as you think it'll be, regardless of how sloppy things are right now."

"That's just it, I believe that promise for two reasons. One, because I know that you'll do whatever you have to do for us to be happy, and two is because when you make promises like that, you can keep them no matter how impossible it seems. And I know the reason behind that has something to do with your past, because you and your brothers get a lot of love from everybody. And you know that I've heard rumors that it's because y'all can't be touched, and that's another reason why I feel like you and Markus are disregarding how Lamar is going to feel or act when he finds out about us."

He now looks away and stares at the floor for a few seconds. "Baby, anybody can be touched regardless of who they are. But we're just fortunate enough to have the mind-set to stay ready to be touched. And we just haven't had any issues that we couldn't handle quietly without one of us actually being seen or heard in a bad way in public. And we do have some special protection surrounding us that we don't talk about, but sometimes we can all still get a little ugly from time to time when necessary. But we're the good guys though, for real baby."

"Stop calling me baby, I said wait until we're official then we can go all in like that!"

We both laugh because I know that he keeps doing it on purpose. He says. "How about I only say baby when it's just us present, and we can talk about your definition of us being 'official' later."

"Okay, but I've never questioned you about any rumors because our friendship isn't based off of that after all of these years. I've truly ignored that part of your life, and I've never wanted to discuss it for several reasons, but you know what my biggest issues were with Lamar as far as my mate. And it's not like I'm not around you and your brothers all the time, so I do hear little comments here and there, but I never ask any questions. But where there's a little smoke there's some fire. I mean all of the rumors can't be all lies, although I've heard so many things that I don't even know what to ask you first. I've even heard that you were some sort of drug kingpin, and that you have like a few million dollars put up somewhere. But Sky told me that she heard that you weren't a kingpin, but she does believe that you have at least one million dollars put up somewhere. But honestly, I think that I would know if you actually had a million dollars stashed away somewhere, so I never really believed that one. And most drug kingpins are well known, and although you're known, I've never heard of you like that as far as drugs. But they say that you never got caught because you never sat still, and while I know that a lot of it isn't true, some of it is. And I know that type of life just doesn't come and go that easily like that, without some real consequences and repercussions."

And while continuing to talk and think of questions, I barely take a breath as I continue.

"So a few questions have to be answered because I just can't see how a person like you could do all of that and stay so unbothered. Because if I've heard all the rumors, then I know that the police and others have heard them, too."

"Listen, baby, when I was young people used to tell me how smart I was all the time. Everywhere I went they would say that I was so smart, but my mom and dad would just ignore it because they were too busy hanging in the streets to notice anything special. But my grandpops saw what they couldn't see, so he got with me and took me under his wings when I was a kid, and the interesting thing about that was that my grandpops had some street hustle in him. But he was the one who was actually a not so street-hustling drug 'lord' who had so much money that even as of today. I still haven't seen nobody hold on to as much money as he was holding on to, because he never really bought anything. It was like he just liked to collect money, and the man stayed so low under the radar that he has never seen the inside of a police station, outside of watching TV, or looking at pictures. So with his skills I'll always refer to him as a Lord. Although you'll never hear his name in the news or in a rap lyric because he wasn't some average street hustler, he actually wasn't street at all. But he was very dangerous, or whatever the word is that's worse than dangerous, and most definitely one of the best to move drugs and so much other shit. He had three top guys who worked for him all of their lives, but they were spread out and under so much control that even if the police did hear anything about them. My grandfather's real name, nor his alias would come up. So he was blessed with their loyalty as they branched out, but he let them take the lead in everything while he stayed in the background watching, so I guess I got my intelligence from him."

He continues with no hesitation. "That's why I've never physically touched anything illegal as far as people know, and I always made sure that nothing could be linked back to me. Ever since the day my grandpops took me into these rooms that were filled with nothing but money, so much money that he eventually had to get a safe house built to store it all in. And I knew right then what I wanted to be when I grew up, especially when he told me that he only let me see it because I wouldn't have fully listened to him if I hadn't seen it with my own eyes. But then he told me that I could potentially make much more money than he's ever made with my brainpower, and I was instantly fascinated that he really thought that I was that smart. So I started believing that I must really be smart for him to show me all the things that he was showing me. I told him that I wanted to know how he made that much money without anybody knowing about it but him and his one friend, Ira, who helped him move it and secure it. Although people did know that he had a little money, but they didn't—and still don't have a clue that he had as much as he did. And while he didn't exactly tell me what he did and how he did it. That same day that he showed me his money, he sat me down and explained to me what, when, and how I could do things without getting robbed, jailed, or killed. Although all of those things are always a possibility no matter who you are or what you do, because nothing can guarantee that it won't happen. But he said that I was smart enough to avoid those things more than the average person. So from that day forward, I told him and myself that I

was going to get money like that one day by using my
brainpower, and that's what I did."

"So you're telling me that you've got some rooms somewhere
filled with money?"

"No, I'm telling you that I ended up getting with him and some
other old heads and strategized my way into setting up a good
life for me and my family—that's all. And as far as the rumors,
people used to say all kinds of things because I was able to
move around from hood to hood without getting caught up in
any territorial bullshit. And that's unheard of because I'd sat
down and thought things out like it was my profession before I
made any moves. I always stayed in the background and was
never seen, but my presence was still very strong in a lot of
places. And my grandpops provided me with money and other
things that my haters didn't have. Even when I had to have
somebody put down, I had to look at it as being a part of my
profession, because I was trying to get paid. And when I had to
disappear and handle things completely solo to get what I
needed, I did whatever I had to do and will never speak about it.
But it's easy to get caught up in the rumors and that lifestyle,
and especially the money because some people don't have a lot
of other options to choose from when it comes to making some
real money. But I had a few other options to choose from, but I
chose to do what I did strictly to collect money, and to not
spend it just like my grandpops did. And I know that we only
saw each other every now and then as teenagers back then. But
if you think back to whenever y'all did see me, I drove the same
car for years. And I never wore much jewelry or designer
clothes or any of that. I still bought things and lived well like I
do now, but I never did too much. Although I did make a few
mistakes as a youngster like we all do, but the old heads kept
my head in the game until I was mature enough to straighten up
and stay focused on my own. That's why a lot of y'all from our

school and our neighborhood didn't see me much until I got older because my grandpops had me doing things that kept me away from my friends back then. But in my maturing, I started to see that I couldn't make that type of living a lifelong thing. Especially one day after seeing how my little brother had shot some guy and then broke his neck over some money that he owed me. And he did it without even asking me if it was okay for him to do it or not, and that's really when that smart shit that my grandpops and everybody else saw in me started to kick in even more. Because I sat back and looked at how much control I had over not only my brothers, but a lot of other men and women who were willing to genuinely look out for me. So I sat back farther and noticed that I could get them to do damn near anything for me, so I asked them to help me shut down everything illegal and give it all up slowly but surely. Because I realized that one of the biggest differences between me and my grandpops, was that his inner circle never grew. But mine did, so I closed myself down and then cleaned up as much money as I could publicly. Before becoming a legit law-abiding citizen for the most part, but yeah. I've influenced a lot of people, and a lot of people have influenced me."

"Wow, Chris, now that's a lot."

"Yeah." He says. "But that doesn't even scratch the surface on why you shouldn't worry about Lamar or nobody else, but for now, hopefully that's enough information to let you know that you'll be financially protected. And even physically protected by not only me, because I would take a bullet for you. But also by some real killers, so just take a little time to let that all soak in before I say anything else."

"Okay." I respond to him while scratching my head.

"It's like I have so much to say right now, but I really don't know what to say right now."

"Don't say anything, let's just let it be what it is for now. While I go back in there and see what's happening with Kris and everybody else. I just wanted to come in here right quick to see if I can come back later, and to also make sure that you are okay after seeing me and Kris in there clowning."

"I'm fine now, I just want to lay down and let my mind process everything that's happening before I receive any more news."

"Aside from that part of my life, you pretty much know absolutely everything else about me already, Chase. I just want you to know that you and the girls will never have to worry about anything, and know that my guys are willing to help me out so that I won't go to prison as far as Lamar or anybody else is concerned. I'll protect you and they'll assist me if I need them to, so don't be worrying about so much all the time. Because although we don't discuss my past, you know that I'm good for the most part of my life now. I run my businesses and keep my guys legitimately working, so I'm straight. I'll personally handle what I need to handle to protect my family, but I still pretty much let the streets take care of the streets."

"I know you do, and thanks for filling me in this much. Although I'm still not satisfied, but I am comfortable and I really can relax a little more now. So we can just pick this conversation back up whenever you come back in here."

"I'm with that."

He says. "I'll get with you later."

164

CHAPTER 20
"HIS LOVE WITH A PRICE"

I've been avoiding checking my phone, but I'd better check it to be sure that my girls haven't called.

I told everybody that I would be out of touch for the next five days, but I'll still keep my phone on just in case of emergencies.

And I see that I have several missed calls and my voice mail box shows that it's full, but none of the calls are from my daughters, so everything must be okay.

Most of the calls are from Lamar, but I don't think that I want to check any of the messages after reading only one of his text messages.

He has already sent me damn near thirty text messages so far, but I'm glad to see that he's the only one who's been blowing up my phone.

Because that means that everyone else must be okay as well, although Indira and Adrian have both called one time. But I can wait to call them back because we'll have plenty of time to chat when I get back home. Because after they find out about all that's happening out here, they're going to be blowing me up in due time, so I'll just wait until then to talk to them.

165

So I just lay my phone down on the nightstand and then search through my things for my sexy pajamas to put on. Then I lay across the bed to take in some meditation time while I finally have some time to myself.

But I fall asleep during my meditation time, because I now turn my head and snatch my phone from the nightstand as I hear it going off.

And I see that I've been laying in this spot for two hours fast asleep and without any interruptions. So that must mean that my phone hasn't rung at all while I slept, nor has anyone knocked on my door within the past two hours. — Or either they've been knocking and calling, but I was literally dead to the world because I haven't heard anything.

But instead of going back to sleep, I'm curious of what everyone else is doing, so I get up to go and check on them.

And at first, I don't see or hear anybody when I come out of my room. Until I faintly hear the pool table balls banging together in the game room.

Sky and Chad must have decided to get in a game of pool before they call it a night because they're still going strong with energy like they aren't sleepy.

"Hey y'all."

I speak while walking into the room with them.

"What's up?"

"Hey, CJ!" Sky responds with a cheesy smile. "We thought that you were in for the night!"

"I thought I was, too. But it had gotten so quiet out here that I thought everybody said fuck it, and just went home."

Laughing, she says. "No you didn't, you just came out here to see where Chris is."

She grins like she can see straight through me and my reason for coming back out here.

"I wasn't looking for him per se, but I do want to know where he is—along with everybody else too."

"He and Markus just went out the front door about ten minutes ago, and Rayci was still in there dealing with Kris. But now I think that she's finally in her room changing and getting ready for bed. But I don't know what Kris is in there doing, Chris went back in there with her for a little while after he came out of your room earlier. But Rayci stayed in there with them the whole time because she didn't want Chris to do anything to Kris if they got into it again."

And now Sky is starting to frown as she begin to tell me how Rayci told her that Kris said that Chris can be with anybody else here on this earth if he doesn't want to be with her, but she will never allow he and I to be together if she has anything to do with it.

"Rayci said that she kept saying that y'all are wrong and that she's going to think of something that will really hurt y'all for doing her like this. That's why Chris got so mad, because he knows how she is."

"She's not going to do anything but get herself fucked up by trying to hurt us by thinking like that!"

I holler while pulling up a chair to take a seat to watch them play.

"And I've already told Chris that I'm not about to be fighting her over this shit every time I see her, and if she's talking about doing something crazy, then she's met her motherfucking match because I'll kill that bitch and they'll never find her body!"

"CJ, you've got bigger problems than Kris."

Chad says while walking in my direction, and putting down his pool stick while taking a seat next to me.

"Lamar has been calling me trying to get me to give you the phone, but I told him that you were sleep since you didn't answer the door when I was knocking on it earlier."

"Man, I was knocked out because I didn't even hear any knocking, I probably would have gotten up and answered the door."

"Nah, it's okay."

He says right before telling Sky to go over and stand by the door, and to tell us if she see anybody coming because he has something to say to me.

"I'm not one to get in the middle of anybody's shit, CJ. And I don't have to tell you that I'm a solid individual who would like to think that if I say something to you. I won't have a problem with you ever repeating it because if I'm keeping everything strictly between us, then so should you. So now, I said that to say that Lamar is really checking for you on some for-real-love type of shit. And although he doesn't get everything right all the time like he wants everyone to think he does, I can say that he loves the hell out of you whether he gets it right or not. And I also know how close you are with my baby, so I got your back. But again, I expect for you to keep what I'm about to tell you strictly between us no matter what. Unless you find out about it some other way—then you can do whatever you want to do with the information, but this conversation still never happened."

"I totally understand, and my words are my bond when I tell you that whatever you're about to say will never be repeated, unless it's repeated by you or Sky."

I now give him my full and undivided attention as he continues.

"All right. Well, a few months ago Lamar and I left y'all at your God-sister's birthday party to go somewhere, but we never came back. Do you remember that?"

"Yeah, I remember."

"Okay, well, Lamar asked me to take him downtown instead of back to his truck. Because he had a meeting with these two lawyers that you don't know about. And when we first got there,

I didn't know what the meeting was about, especially at such an odd time of the day on a Saturday. I just knew that one of the lawyers was the same lawyer that he had recommended to my cousin when he needed one a while ago. But then he started telling me about how his mom was always stealing money from him, and how much he can't trust her. He told me how you are the only person that he's ever been able to fully trust for real, even when you're mad at him. And that's why we were there, because he took his mom's name off of his life insurance policy as his beneficiary, and put yours on there. I think he has a Last Will and Testament and everything, he said that y'all will probably end up married if y'all can ever stop breaking up over the same shit all the time. And he gave them all of your information, your full name, date of birth, and even your damn social security number. I'm not sure of what all he gave them, but I'm positive that he provided them with whatever they needed about you. And no disrespect, CJ, but after he told me how much you would be getting if something ever happened to him. I told him that no female, not even you should be getting that kind of money before you walk down that aisle and say 'I do' first. And y'all don't even have kids together yet, but he still redid his will and even recorded it to make sure that you will be okay if anything ever happens to him, and I'm not sure if he removed his mom from everything completely. But you're definitely his main beneficiary, and since he doesn't have kids. None of his family, including his mom has no power to stop you from getting it."

"This is just too much."

I utter in fear as my heart begins to speed up, while I think about how Lamar is going to feel when he finds out about me and Chris.

"What I don't understand is why would he put me down as his beneficiary without saying anything to me first? Even if his momma doesn't deserve it, he has plenty of other family members!"

"I told you why he did it, he said that he loves you and that he thinks that he's going to end up marrying you anyway."

Chad says. "No matter how many times y'all break up, he always say that he can't be who you want him to be right now. But he knows that you love him and he can trust you."

"Now ain't that some shit."

I sigh while longing to just get away.

"Now I'm not going to tell you how much you'll be getting because you would definitely have him killed today!"

He laughs and now tells me that he will be calling Lamar in the morning to see where he's at, so that he won't just come popping back up out here with everything being the way it is right now.

"I'll do my best in keeping you posted on his whereabouts, but if he calls you then you may want to answer. I told you everything that I just told you because I know that it will help you to see how much he really loves you, so just be careful. But like I said, you may want to answer your phone to keep him from coming back and walking up on all of this shit that y'all got going on out here."

"Okay, I'll go and get my phone so that I can answer it the next time he calls. But I don't know what to say to him, I mean don't get me wrong. I do love Lamar, and he will always have a place in my heart. But I don't have much to say to him anymore because I truly am in love with Chris, and I don't have to question it or anything like that. It's like I've finally realized that we are a perfect fit for each other after all this time. So it'll be weird talking to Lamar right now, especially after knowing that he has put me down as his beneficiary. That makes me not want to talk to him even more, because I'm already kind of scared of what's going to happen when he finds out about me

and Chris as it is. Because I know that he's going to think the same way as Kris does, when it's not even like that at all. Because seriously, Chad. I really do think that I probably would have ended up marrying Lamar one day if he hadn't cheated."
I continue while shaking my head and still feeling nervous.
"And if all of this other stuff between me and Chris wouldn't have happened, maybe we could've worked through it with counseling or something. Because if I didn't trust my family, or didn't have any kids. I honestly love and trust Lamar enough to put him down as my beneficiary as well. But we've never talked about anything like that, not even when we do get into our discussions about marriage."
"Well, before I came knocking on your door, I told him that I've been spending the majority of my time locked in the bedroom with Sky. Because I didn't want to answer any more of his questions about how you're feeling or what you're doing."
He says. "But I don't think that he'll come at Chris as much as he'll come at you because you're the one that he was in a relationship with. But since he can't get to you without going through Chris, I think you should just try to keep them apart until we get back home. Because if he comes back out here, Kris is definitely going to tell him about y'all whether you like it or not, and although Lamar's not going to run up on a guy like Chris. And Chris probably won't run up on Lamar either, but all of that shit can quickly change right before your eyes if you don't get in front of it right now."
"I know, that's why I'm going to figure something out before I let that happen."
"Shh, here they come."
Sky says while continuing to sit in the doorway like she's just sitting there because she wants to, and not because she's our lookout person.
"Why are you sitting on the floor?"

Chris asks her while he and Markus wait for her to move so that they can come into the room with us.

"We're playing truth or dare again, but Chris you can't play! Your truths be starting up way too much shit, so I dare you to just go over there and have a seat and not join us!"

We all laugh as she gets up and walk back over to pick up her pool stick, just as Chad does so that they can finish their game.

"Where have y'all been?"

I now direct my attention to Chris and Markus.

"Y'all are always disappearing together, what's up?"

"I had some business that I had to handle before I called it a night."

Chris answers while coming to take a seat next to me. "Business, what kind of business do you have to handle way out here in these sticks? There's nobody out here but us. Wait, you know what, Chris. Don't answer that. What's important is that we have that talk that we spoke about earlier, and I guess since we're not doing anything, there's no time like the present for you to tell me whatever else that you feel that I should know."

"Let me get cleaned up, and we can spend the rest of the night together."

He says. "As you can see, I still haven't showered since I left your room earlier, so I'm about to go into Markus and Rayci's room to shower. Then I'm coming straight to wherever you are when I'm done."

"I'll be out here waiting for you because I'm not going back to sleep anytime soon. And if Sky and Chad end up going to bed or anything, then I'll be out on the deck waiting for you."

"Okay that's cool."

He now asks them. "Do y'all know if Rayci is still in there with Kris?"

"No, she's not in there."

Sky answers.

"She told us that she was about to get ready for bed, so I'm guessing that she's already in there showering, and Kris still never came out of y'alls room yet. I don't know why she's in there acting like she can't come out of that room, it's not like we don't already know how we all are after a fight."

"That's just how Kris is, she'll come out after she's had time to process everything that's inside of her head. The only thing about her is which level will she be on whenever she does come out is what's going to be the factor in how things will be. But I called Chauncey already and told him to go over to our house first thing in the morning to take out everything that belongs to me."

"What?"

I shout loudly. "Why, Chris?"

"Because I have to, if I don't cut all ties with her as far as us living together goes, then things are only going to get worse between us now that she's found out how I really feel. And she's not going to be the same after this anyway, so my brothers need to go on over there and take out everything that I asked them to take out before we get back."

"Damn, Chris. You're not wasting any time are you?"

Sky says. "She's going to be mad as hell when she gets home and your stuff isn't there. But you're right to cut all ties with her because I have never seen you get that mad at her before, I thought that you was about to put her ass to sleep tonight."

"Later for all of that shit."

He says calmly and without jest. "She can have the house, the furniture, and plenty of money to spend. But I can't have my son seeing me mad at her all the time because we're always arguing and fighting about something in front of him. Anyway, that's over." He now hits me on my leg all playful like he's trying to loosen things up.

173

"It must be nice to be able to just move out of your crib overnight like that and arrange for things to be in order for you when you get back home, but Kris and I will be going to war with our boxing gloves strapped on when we get back. And I know that you can protect me or whatever, but excuse me if I'm not flattered by your touch right now—for real."

"I told you that you're not going home to all of that."

He says. "That's the other reason why I'm moving my things— so that I can be more accessible to you for whenever you need me. Because I'm going to tell Kris that I moved out when I take her home tomorrow, but she shouldn't be too surprised because it's not like we haven't been talking about it for the past few weeks. I've just been too busy taking care of the party, so I haven't had time to do any moving. But I told her weeks ago that I was moving out, way before either of you knew how I was feeling about you. I already knew that I had to move out regardless of whether you were with Lamar or not, just like I know that I can't go back to living with her after this. And until you and Lamar are squared away, I need to be available to you 24/7, and able to leave and do whatever I want to do by living with you or by myself without having her running behind me trying to see what I'm doing. But don't keep worrying about her because she's already got out most of her frustration. Usually once Kris has had time to blow off some steam, she's easier to deal with, it's going to take some time but we'll all be fine.

"It's not Kris that I'm worried about, because I can handle her myself. It's Lamar who I'm worried about because if you think that we're having a hard time convincing Kris that we haven't been creeping this whole time, I'm positive that he's not going to want to hear any form of reasoning when he finds out about us. He'll definitely think that we've been creeping behind his back, and it's going to be all bad, Chris."

"If y'all aren't together anymore then there's not much that he can say or do about any of this, and he can't do anything about what's happened in the past because the last time I checked. You were single when he left here to go home, right?"

"Technically, yeah. I guess."

"Okay, but you're my girl now, since we've somewhat laid it out like that. And I can't have you walking around here all shook up thinking that he's going to do something to us because we're together. So I may need to be the one to speak with him from this day forward instead of you anyway, because you're right—there will be no reasoning. So I'm not sure if I feel comfortable with you talking to him by yourself."

"What's up y'all?"

Rayci catches our attention by abruptly strutting threw the door with a smile on her face.

"What are y'all in here doing?"

She comes over and pulls up a seat next to Markus.

"Chris, I just knocked on your bedroom door. But Kris didn't answer. I think she may have gone to sleep, so maybe she'll be in a better mood when she wakes up."

"Yeah," I respond. "That or she'll be revived and ready to start round two with me."

"Don't listen to her."

Chris says. "I fucked up thinking that we could handle it together, but I've learned my lesson. Now I know to keep them apart so there will be no more fighting. But thanks for checking on her again for me, now I can go into y'alls room and get cleaned up. I'll be back out here in a minute."

He now gets up to go and take a shower while Sky and Chad stop their game again.

Sky comes over to mingle with me and Rayci while Chad leaves the room right behind Chris and Markus.

Sky says. "I really do want to sit here and talk to y'all but my man is ready to go to bed, so I'll see you chicks tomorrow. He said that he's ready for Sky to take him to the sky tonight baby!"

"I knew that y'all were going to leave me hanging sooner or later anyway, so go on and enjoy your man, Skylar. We'll see you in the morning because I know that Rayci is going to be leaving me hanging in a minute too, watch. Markus is going to put Chris out after he takes that shower, then I won't see neither of you again until in the morning."

I say this with a smile on my face while honestly in my heart feeling happy to see that my drama hasn't completely messed up this entire trip for everybody.

"Girl, please!"

Sky says. "You will not be out here by yourself because Chris is about to be on you like white on rice when he comes out. And I hope you talk to him for real about all of this because Lamar is going to be so upset, and Chris needs to get back to being his usual precise self, before we have to handle this shit ourselves. Because I feel like he knew that you and Kris had to fight at least once just to get it out of the way, because he normally wouldn't have put such a drama filled situation in the same room like that, talking about he didn't think it through."

"Right!"

Rayci agrees with her. "Chris thinks everything through!"

"I just know that he needs to fix it before we do, because I don't mind doing whatever I have to do to help you stay protected after Lamar finds out about y'all."

Being her normal honest self, Sky steps up to the plate by unequivocally having my back like I have hers.

She says. "And CJ, I'm so serious because Chris is acting like everything is going to be OK, when it's not!"

"I feel you Sky, I really do. But I believe that he's going to handle his part as far as stopping things before it gets out of control again, because you may be right about how he handled me and Kris. Because he does think too far ahead to allow all of that to happen the way that it did, but I also knew that it needed to happen as well. But now that Chris and I are communicating on the level that we're on now. I feel like Lamar may not actually be as big of a problem as we may think. But ultimately, I'm still going to have to straighten this shit out myself. And I love you and Chris for stepping up but I got this. I just need to go in there and get my phone so that I can try to stop Lamar from coming back out here."

"Are you still going to be communicating with Lamar while you're with Chris?"

Rayci says. "Because if you are, then you'd better not let Chris hear you talking to him on the phone or anything. Especially if you've already told him that you're completely done with Lamar."

"Oh, he's not going to be able to hear me if he's in the shower, but he's not dumb. I'm sure he knows that Lamar has been blowing up my phone, and at this point. I will be talking to Lamar whenever he calls me, at least for now I will. But I'm going to talk to Chris about all of this when he comes back out here, because I'm not about to be secretly doing stuff behind his back like y'all be doing with y'all men."

We all burst into laughter because they know what I mean, then I get up to go and get my phone so that I can hear it if it rings while I wait for Chris.

And it doesn't take me but a few minutes to go into my room to get my phone before I come back to see that Sky and Rayci have both already left to go and be with their men, and it's cool because now I can go out onto the deck and enjoy some personal thinking time that's still needed anyway.

CHAPTER 21
"WHO ARE YOU REALLY"

As time pass while I sit on the deck and wait for Chris. I stand up and gaze at the beautiful trees and take in some more fresh air.

Soon I hear a voice coming in behind me singing.

"Look at that booty, yeah—I want that booty."

"How can you be thinking about booty when we've got so much crap going on out here Chris?"

"I know that we have a lot to think about, but that doesn't mean we can't get busy and keep making up for lost times first. We can talk after we finish touching on each other again."

"We can touch on each other and everything like that, but we're going to have to make sure that we have a conversation or two before daylight for real."

He now proceeds to grab my hand and direct me to follow him.

"Okay, that's cool. So come on and let's go and take a walk so that we can be alone again."

I now grab my phone and a bottle of water before we leave the deck to go outside of the cabin to get away from everybody.

He says. "Until we've walked far enough from the cabin, we can talk and catch up if you want to just ask me whatever else that you want to know about me that you don't already know."

"I want to know everything. I mean honestly, I have questions on top of questions when it comes to you and how you lived your life before we became as close as we are now. And I won't let anything that you tell me affect the relationship that we have now because of how much I love you. But I'm not about to stay in the dark about your background now that my heart and love for you is viewed in a different way than before. I want to know the same Chris as Poolo and the other guys know. Because although you've told me a lot, I already knew that they don't call you all of those nicknames for nothing, and major respect is always given to you like you can't be dealt with like any ole Joe Blow from the streets. And I've been around when you've mentioned how it seems like you'd already traveled a great portion of this world by the time you were twenty years old. But you never said why or how you were able to do that other than because of your grandfather's job, but after hearing how he took you under his wings. I now understand that part a little better because you would always give me a weird look and change the subject anytime we would talk about your grandfather, but now I understand why you were so close."

I now pause for a second before saying.

"But I also thought that maybe it was because he's passed away, so you just didn't like to talk about him."

"You wanted to stay in the dark about my past, so it was hard for me to talk to you about him due to that. And I do have my days when I won't talk about him to anyone, but I don't want you to be in the dark so I'm open to it. But like I said earlier, I'm not sure what all you've heard already, because people be making up all kind of shit about me being some kind of notorious street king."

179

He says. "One time my mom told me that somebody called and told her that the police was even scared of me. And you know that's a lie because at the end of the day, those motherfuckers ain't scared of nobody. But that's why you can't believe everything you hear, because if that was true, then I would've been on their narcotic radar a long time ago. But I will tell you that the true part to some of the rumors is that my money is long, and I don't scare easily. And that's how I was able to build a name but no name for myself in a few different areas, after I decided to leave my grandpops and come back home from the Island's to permanently do my own thing. And I already had people in motion, so word got out and they saw that I did whatever I had to do to get whatever I needed. Regardless of who I was dealing with, I laid down whoever I had to before I got wiser and hired some heavy hitters to hold things down for me when my brothers couldn't do it. I just made sure to keep absolutely everything very temporary no matter where I went."

He says. "People didn't know exactly who I was or what my real name was at that time, because I stayed under the radar and moved around so much. But they started calling me whatever they wanted to call me, but nobody ever really saw my face. And if they did see me, it was never good for anybody involved, so most of the time I was never contacted. But like I said people were always guessing my identity, and with the help of my grandpops, here in the States things started working in my favor in all kinds of ways. I was able to mastermind my way into a lot of street money once I started recruiting a few more mature hungry heads that were willing to do whatever I wanted them to do to get paid. I just made sure to always use my brainpower to cover my ass and make sure that nothing could ever be linked back to me or my family."

He continues as we continue to walk. "Because like I said, my grandpops and Ira introduced me to drugs and money when I was barely a teenager, so I knew a lot. And I was hanging in the streets with my brother's way before my teenage years, so all of that somewhat helped prepared me for all that I saw my grandpops and Ira doing. Although there was nothing that could really prepare a kid for the things that I saw when I was with them. Because it seemed like they always forgot how old I was, because eventually they didn't hide anything from me. I pretty much heard and saw whatever they heard and saw, no matter what it was about. And I loved it because I learned a lot. And I was able to spend just as much time growing up in the Caribbean's with them, just as I did here in the States. They would let me go just about everywhere with them, until it was time for me to come back home for school, and you would think that my brothers and I grew up a little differently than our homies. Because we had both parents living under the same roof with us, but you know we didn't. Because even when they were trying to raise us right, they couldn't do it because they were constantly trying to avoid each other, so we ended up being neglected. And that's why we became some of the worst kids in our neighborhood for a little while. And I'm sure you heard about how bad we were, because we used to see y'all hanging out at the park all the time before we had gotten to know each other. Everybody knew that we were bad as fuck, but then when I got old enough to move things around like I wanted to. I got with my brothers to make sure that all of them got cleaned up and ready to get right. Even the two who are older than me got on board and did whatever they had to do to get paid. And as my blood brothers we all know what we all can and can't tolerate as a unit, so once I got them set up. I just bounced back and forth from the Caribbean's to the States because I just couldn't sit still. On top of me just having genuine love for my grandpops and Ira, because it was like Ira was my daddy, and my grandpops was just always my grandpops. Ira looked out for me like I was his son because he taught me just as much as my grandpops did. Sometimes the teachings were never good in terms of how to take the straight and narrow road in doing things legally. I had to teach myself a lot of the legal stuff, but I took everything that they taught me for what it was worth. And now that my pops can see how I turned out, he be trying to step up and be a father nowadays, but it's too late for all of that now. But my brothers and I all still try to maintain whatever father-and-son relationships that we can with him, since he's trying. Because when I first started hustling, I did a lot of things out of my parents crib for a long time, and I think they knew what I was doing. But they didn't give a shit because nobody was asking them for anything, and now that he and my mom have finally decided to stop running the streets and stop cheating on each other, we all basically just stay out of their relationship and let them do whatever it is that they're going to do. Especially since they're trying to be good grandparents, they've been stepping up by trying to make up for their absence in our lives by being there for our kids, so I guess it's cool. And while you already know about my parents and my childhood, we've never really gotten deep into me telling you how I just took it upon myself to look to Ira and my grandpops to show me how to make that big money like they were making, so that I could help my brothers. But then I soon started taking care of everybody, and my brothers knew that all I wanted in return was for them to stay clean and to get a job or something to help themselves stay out of trouble. And some of them knuckleheads listened to me, and for some of them it took a minute to it get right, but now we're all good for the most part. Even the hardest one of us all started treating me like I was the father of our family, and now Chauncey is one of the more responsible ones. You only know the Chauncey that he is now, but that dude was a beast and we all knew that he was going to end up dead or in prison for sure.

And he knew it too, but he didn't care, so he definitely has one of the biggest turn around stories regarding his life and our family. But we've all been walking this legal line for a while now, although I still keep a steady eye on certain things. But that's just an old habit that I picked up from Ira and my grandpops. I never get too comfortable to the point to where I stop watching my own back, even when I'm paying somebody else to watch it for me. Everything around me is straight, but I keep my eyes opened like I'm out here all by myself, and that's just a habit that I'll probably always have."

"Wow, Chris, it's kind of weird to find out that some of the things that were in my head are true. But something's I've been way off with how I thought they were, but I honestly knew that all of that respect wasn't being given to you because you have big-name clients and stuff. Because when somebody would call you MC, when I know those aren't your initials. I would ignore it on purpose because I knew that it had something to do with your background. So you're the man, huh?"

I state while laughing, and with my hands on my hips.

But he laughs with me and says.

"You already know I'm the man—your man. And I would have told you all of this a long time ago. But I'm glad that we've finally had this conversation now, hopefully it will help you to understand what I mean when I tell you not to worry about things. My life goes far beyond what meets the eye, and I got you."

"I know that you've got me. And there were a lot of questions that I had, but now you've pretty much answered everything and it sums it all up. So I'm cool with that, and since I've heard a few people call you MC, I want to know if I can call you that sometimes, too?"

"Hell no, you can't call me that!"

He says. "I won't answer if you call me any nicknames that you've heard them calling me!"

I now begin to chuckle.

"I wouldn't call you any of those names anyway. I was just messing with you, but I do want to know what does MC mean?"

"They say that it stands for Money Chris, but my brothers say that it stands for Millionaire Chris, because some of them know that I was making truckloads of money. But I never really bought anything, so they think that I've got some major stacks put up somewhere or something. Regardless of my companies, and no matter how successful I am, they always try to put their own little puzzles together on where did all of that money go? Since my businesses pretty much pay for themselves, but they'll never figure that shit out. I make a lot of money from my businesses and I live my life comfortably and at my own pace, so everybody can just keep guessing for all I care. I still avoid any unnecessary spending even now with our increase and lucrative flow of recent customers. And I will always keep my eyes open in case one day somebody near or far decides to jump stupid and try to rob me to see how long my money really is. But I just want you to know that I got all of that under control, so you can relax and stop worrying about you and the girls' safety so much. Everything will be fine because if I do just so happen to have one million or several millions. Then that means that you just so happen to have one million or several millions. And if I'm still walking around here safe, then that means that you and our kids will still be walking around here safe."

"That's what's up, Chris. And I get it, but I want to know what all does Kris know about your past that she can use against you right now?"

"Kris knows things, but nothing that she can really use against me. You know way more than she does even without the information that I just gave you. You still know more than what

I've told her, but I'm not worried about her. I mean she may have her issues and everything like that, but Kris knows not to bring up anything like that at all concerning me. That's like a death sentence in my eyes, no matter who you are. And she knows that, but even if she decides to one day say fuck it. And try to ruin me, she can't. So now, how about we change this conversation and pick it up another time, so that we can focus on each other for a while?"

"Okay, that's cool with me."

CHAPTER 22
"ALL BAD NEWS"

It seems like Chris and I have been walking for a mile or two before we make it to the lake.

The lake that will soon become one of our favorite spots out here, because he's got me horny all over again with his wisdom and knowledge when it comes to understanding when enough is enough as far as getting money however you can. Then flipping it to make it work for you. And with me knowing that I won't have to constantly worry about him and his lifestyle, this makes me want him even more because he really does get it.

He can already comprehend everything that I was continuously trying to get Lamar to see when it comes to turning his life around.

"Chris, I'm glad that you decided to handle your business and move on to a more secure lifestyle. That's all that I be talking about when I come to you discussing or complaining about Lamar's ways of life. So I must say that it's turning me on that you already have your shit together without me having to force you to do it, and it has me fighting to keep my legs closed now that I fully know what kind of man that I have in front of me right now."

"Well, damn, if it's making you feel that way then I wish I would have told you all of this a long time ago!"
"It's making me super horny."
"Good."
He says while smiling. "Because I've been waiting a long time to have you all to myself like this."
He now takes his T-shirt off so that I can sit down on it, but I grab him by his arm to pull him down and close to me as soon as I sit down to view the lake.
And I don't hesitate to place a kiss upon his lips, and I love how he kisses me back before hijacking the situation and straddling me. — He now places his hands all over my body as if he can't wait to feel me again, while our tongues and lips glide until he reaches to take off my top.
He now grabs my breasts and grips them like he owns them, but still not too forceful or eager because although he's anxious. He's taking things slow and allowing me to take in everything that he's putting out right now. Even as he dips down and starts sucking and licking on my nipples, while I lay back and admire his sexiness.
And as we get more into each other, I decide to reach for my bottled water and pull his hands so that he can stand to his feet, while I stand up with him.
I now drink from the bottle while leaving some of the water in my mouth, and I drop to my knees and let his dick submerge into the water like a submarine, until the water is gone.
Then I drink some more while leaving even more water in my mouth this time, so that I can really drown his dick in it. I also dunk his balls in and out of the water a few times as I gradually stroke and jack his dick and listen to him moan. So I continued to refill my mouth and continue to have a dunk contest between his dick and his balls after he's able to stand back upright after tilting over.

And I don't neglect his dick head because I let it get in a few splashes before I rinse out my mouth and use my shirt as a towel.

And now as we add to his T-shirt and whatever other pieces of clothing that we can comfortably take off and put on the ground so that we can lay on them.

We begin to repeat what happened earlier in the bedroom because he immediately goes down and begins to lunch on me like he just can't get enough.

And my legs begin to shake while my toes curl in so hard that it feels like I've broken at least four toes already.

So I just lay back while at the same time trying to pull myself together before I really do break a toe or pop a blood vessel or something, because Chris is awesome at what he's doing.

But I eventually pull him up to me so that he can let his dick guide itself straight into me. While he slowly moves in and out of me as the consistent passion that we have for each other comes forward.

And with the combination of his roll and thrust, mixed with my roll and thrust. I just sink my nails into his back while trying not to hurt him because he has me feeling the need to sink my nails into something.

And since it won't be into the dirt, his back is where my hands keep landing, as he's making love to me good and sturdy.

Got me feeling like I really should have been letting him do me slow and hard like this way before now for real.

And the fact that his big dick isn't making me want to just stop everything and get up is impressive, especially when he opens my legs wide enough so that we both can look down at our body parts and see the penetration with a good view of how much we're fulfilling our desires to please each other like nothing else matters.

It's all very intriguing.

And while daylight is starting to break through, I get on top of him and give him a few grips and dips while he's plunged all the way inside of me until he climaxes pretty quickly after that.

And after we're done, we just lay still and hold each other once again, and I just close my eyes and take it all in.

I'm relaxing on a cloud that I don't want to get off of again, but eventually I have to because the actual clouds in the sky are becoming brighter by the minute. — So I nudge Chris to make sure that he's awake, so that we can get ourselves together and head back to the cabin before everybody gets up.

And as we make our journey back to the cabin, we get in some serious chatting time, and it includes me explaining to him how much I love him. Although that doesn't mean that the love that I have for Lamar just disappeared.

"I love Lamar but it's nothing in comparison to what we have. And I can love him from a distance because romantically there is nothing anymore, and there will never be anything more at this point. I just don't want to lie to you and act like our stuff just disappeared, because it was never love if I could just drop my feelings like that. But I need for you to know that he and I will never ever have anything romantically again, and it's not even because he cheated on me. It's because I love and respect you way too much to try to bounce back and forth, especially when I know that you're fully committed to me and us."

"I guess I can understand that, but if you think that y'all are going to be able to be friends. Then you can think again because at the end of the day, no matter what's happening between us. He's going to always want more, just like I did."

And it seems that we will have to continue this discussion later, because we now quickly approach the cabin and can smell breakfast being cooked as soon as we walk through the door. And it's right on time because my stomach is growling.

Rayci is the first person that we see when we walk inside.

189

"It's almost seven o'clock!"
She says. "Where are y'all coming from looking all musty?"
We all laugh while I tell her that we decided to just sleep outside so that we could be alone without any interruptions.
"I see. Well, I made a little breakfast for everybody since I'm so used to getting up to cook for Markus and the kids. It's such a habit that I couldn't stop thinking about all the breakfast food that we brought with us. So I had to come in here and at least cook us all some bacon and eggs, but there's also some fruit, oatmeal, bagels, and cream cheese over there if you want that instead."
"Okay."
"I'm about to get some orange juice and fix me a plate!"
Chris says while washing his hands before pouring himself a glass of orange juice.
"Rayci, did you guys come back out of your room at all after y'all left me?"
"Nope, that was it for me. I went in and didn't come back out until this morning."
She says, "Markus came out one time to get something to drink, but after that it was lights-out for us."
"Good morning, everybody."
Sky says while walking into the kitchen yawning, and wearing some big bunny slippers.
"Why in the hell are y'all up so damn early?"
She complains while also looking around like she's just as happy as we are to see that Rayci has gotten up and made breakfast.
"Y'all woke me up with all of this noise in here!"
"We did not wake you up because we're not even loud, and these walls are too thick. You probably just smelled this food and couldn't go back to sleep. So you might as well just come on over here and fix yourself a plate like everybody else."

"Is Chad up, too?"

"Kind of."

She answers. "He said a few words to me when I told him that I was about to get up and come in here. But then he turned back over and put the covers over his head after I got up, so I don't know if he's in there sleep or what. How long have y'all been up?"

"I've been up for almost an hour." Rayci answers. "Well, actually more like an hour in a half."

"And I haven't really been to sleep for real because Chris and I have been up talking and trying to figure things out."

"Yeah right, you know that we don't believe that y'all were up just talking. But okay, I guess Kris and I are the only late bloomers this morning. Or has she already been out here, too?" Sky questions while opening the refrigerator to get out some milk.

"Nope." Rayci responds. "She hasn't come out yet, or at least not since I've been up."

"Chris, you probably should go and knock on the door and tell her to bring her ass on out of there!"

Sky says. "She's had time to sleep all of that shit off just like the rest of us, and I can help y'all figure this all out if you want me to because my brain is fresh and ready to help this morning."

"Nah, we're good."

Chris says while shaking his head. "We don't need for you to figure anything out for us Dr. No, we got this."

He says. "She's not going to stay in there all day anyway, because she's going home today now that she's had time to calm down and get herself together. I'm sure that I'll be the only one who will have to deal with her today, so please just let her take her time in coming out here."

"I'm sorry, Chris. But I'm about to go and knock on the door and ask her if she wants some breakfast, because she's gotta be hungry."

Rayci declares as she now walks out of the kitchen and over to the bedroom door to knock on it.

"Damn, is she in there?" She yells after about a minute of knocking without getting an answer.

But she continues to knock even harder, but still she receives no answer.

"It's locked!" She says while turning the knob to try to open it, after quite a few more knocks.

And now she's calling Kris's name to get up to come and open the door, but there's still no answer.

"This girl probably hasn't come out of this room all night!" Rayci begins to panic. "And I hope that there's nothing wrong in there! Chris, will you please come and tell her to open the door, please?"

"Nah." He says nonchalantly like he just knows that there's nothing wrong with her.

"She don't want to be bothered so just leave her alone, she'll come out in a minute. Because she can't still be in there sleep after all of that beating you just did!"

"Well, Markus is going to have to get up and come and make her open this damn door! Because I think something's wrong! I'm sorry, but even if he has to break it open, we're getting into this got-damn room if she don't answer it by the time I get back!"

She now leaves to go and get Markus.

"Break it open!"

Chris says while walking over to the big entrance of the kitchen to get a better view of her walking down the hallway to go and get Markus.

"We're not about to break or knock over anything else in this place! I'm the one who's going to have to answer to these people about their property, not y'all! So I'll go in there after I finish eating, because I know that she's up after all of that knocking and yelling!"

Rayci still proceeds to go and get Markus to come and help her, especially now that she believes that something is wrong.

And when Markus finally comes out to help her, he gets no response either.

"Kris, please come and open this door so that Ray can leave me alone!"

He says with his eyes barely opened, after tampering with the doorknob himself.

"It's too damn early for this shit, what in the hell is she in there doing?"

He continues to knock and twist on the doorknob, just as Rayci was doing earlier.

"Something's wrong!"

Rayci shouts in a panic. "Now y'all know that she would've come to this damn door by now if she was just in there asleep!"

And by her and Chris taking the first bedroom down the hallway when we first got here, like they always do.

Sky, Chris, and I all have a good view from the kitchen area due to that. And we can all see and hear everything that's happening without even having to walk all the way over to the entrance to see that she's really not responding to either of them.

So finally, Chris decides to walk closer to help them out.

"Kris, if we have to break open this door! I'm going to be mad as hell because you know you can say something to let us know that you're okay!"

Then after he receives no response, his frustration seems to quickly turn into concern as well, judging by the expressions on his face.

"Kris!"

He shouts and now beat on the door a few more times. "Somebody bring me a knife or something so that I can open this motherfucking door!"

He now picks at the lock with his hands, trying to open it without a key.

"Damn, just kick it open, Chris!"

Rayci sputters with fear. "Please kick it open because something is wrong! I'm telling y'all that something's wrong!"

And at this point we are all now worried about the situation. Even I can sense that something is wrong because she's not answering the door for anybody, not even Chris.

So Sky and I get up to try to help them get into the room to check on her. But Chris grabs the doorknob and leans into the door really hard with his shoulder a few times, breaking it open. And as we all go inside, we can see that the window is open, but we don't see Kris.

The mattress is stripped of its coverings, and a trail of linens and clothing is tied to the expensive bedpost, leading out of the window.

And we all rush over to the window only to see Kris's body dangling from the homemade rope, with one of Chris's t-shirts ripped and made into a rope around her neck.

She has tied and tightened all of the fabrics together and apparently roped them tight enough around the bedpost, and around her neck to hold her there after she jumped out of the window.

Shocked and appalled, we all cry out loud. Especially after Sky, Rayci, and I witness Markus trying to stop Chris from pulling her up. When we can clearly see that her color has completely changed and her body is definitely hanging lifeless.

"You can't touch this shit, Chris! Stop!"

Markus shouts as he wrestles with him.

"Somebody call the police and the security house so that they can come and see this shit for themselves, after all that's happened out here! Don't touch her!"

"I can't just leave her hanging out there like this, we have to pull her up!" Chris now fall to his knees and lean out of the window and starts pulling her back inside anyway.

While he's crying down to her saying something that I can't hear due to the fact that I have to run into the bathroom because I'm just too overwhelmed. So I don't know if he pulled her all the way back inside or not, but I think he did because he kept saying that couldn't just leave her there. I just know that Sky ran to get Chad, and to call the police.

While I almost knock Rayci over as I'm trying to make it to the bathroom sink, because I feel like I'm about to pass out if I don't get some cold water onto my face immediately.

"I'm sorry, Kris! I'm so sorry!"

I cry out while I hover over the sink in sorrow after splashing water onto my face.

"Oh my God, I'm so sorry, Kris!"

All I can think of is if I hadn't fallen for Chris, then maybe she wouldn't have done this to herself.

"CJ, this isn't your fault!"

Rayci sobs while coming in behind me and handing me a dry towel for me to wipe my face and hands with.

"Nobody knew that she was feeling this way!"

"Why would she do this? It's not that serious!"

I continue to cry out as Rayci and I both just hold each other.

"Why would she go this far?"

I now bury my head into her chest and weep like a baby, and she weeps back.

I feel shocked and afraid, and maybe most of all hurt that she would ever take things this far knowing that they have a son who will need his mother.

195

Sky soon comes running into the bathroom, and holding my cell phone as well as hers, while crying and asking us if we're going to be okay.

And we all just continue to cry and mourn together before we eventually exit the bathroom.

"Chad, will you go and flush that weed and anything else that we brought that needs to be flushed away before the police get here?"

We now witness Markus talking to Chad while still standing next to Chris, who looks every bit of distraught and hurt as he sit staring at Kris. As if his mind isn't present with us right now, and I want to just run over to him and give him a big hug. And let him know that I am here for him to lean on, but I'm guessing that's not such a good idea right now.

"Should I go over there to be with Chris?"

I say to Sky and Rayci before we leave the room. "Look at him, he looks like he's going to lose his mind if I don't. I can't even imagine what's going on inside of his head right now."

"No, CJ, that's why Markus is staying with him. Let's try to work on getting you together first."

Sky says while handing me my phone.

"So come on and follow me into another room, or let's just go outside or somewhere."

I now look at Chris again, in hopes of him maybe looking at me at least one time before we walk out.

But he doesn't, he just cries while gazing at the floor and grabbing his dreads as he rocks back and forth.

And the security house workers pull up about five minutes after Sky called them to let them know what's happened.

And only a short while after that, the cabin is filled with plenty of cops and detectives, and I want nothing more than to just run away from it all.

"Do you want to go outside or stay in here?"

Sky asks, as we slowly walk around to the table that we were previously about to eat on.

"I think I'm going to have to go outside because everything about this cabin has me feeling like I no longer want to be inside of here ever again."

I answer her while watching a female detective walk over to us and say. "Excuse me ladies, but can either of you tell me anything about why Ms. Johnson's neck, face, and arms have so many injuries?"

And my first thought is to just take off running because this can't go anywhere but downhill for me.

And although the front door is wide open, there's nothing but law enforcement people walking in and out trying to find out what all happened, so I know that I won't get too far.

"Okay listen. I'm just going to be honest with you, detective. She's been in a few fights out here with multiple people, but some of her injuries came from me because we'd gotten into a fight last night. But I had no idea that she was feeling suicidal, I mean I would have never fought her if I would've known that she was hurting that bad inside."

And as I continue to explain what happened, I stay honest with her about everything, even making sure to show her where she had bitten me on my arm.

But now I begin to cry as I explain how I really would have never in a million years thought that she would do this to herself.

"I wish that we would have never fought, but I can't change it now."

I cry more, while regretting everything as I get all worked up again.

"It's very unfortunate, some things just happen beyond our control."

"I know, and I'm sorry, but may I be excused? I have to get some fresh air."

"Sure."

The detective says. "I would like to get some photos of your injuries, but I can come out there to take the photos."

"Okay, that's fine."

I now walk away from her and go straight outside to get away from it all, while she goes to get her camera.

And finally when I make it outside, Chris walks over to me and ask.

"Where have you been?"

He says. "I've been looking for you to let you know that I haven't been neglecting you, I just need to be by myself for a while. So try not to take anything that I say or do out of context."

And now he literally turns around and walks away from me without even giving me a chance to respond to him.

And I just stand still and watch him walk away from me without even trying to force him to say more.

But the tears that were already coming from my eyes when he was talking, are now streaming down my face even more because I could hear and see his pain.

And there is absolutely nothing that I can do about it besides stay out of his way. Although I'm still going to stay near him and be available for him for whenever he does need me.

Because ultimately, we're all going to need each other because this is a lot to take in for all of us.

CHAPTER 23
"A TIME TO TELL"

I take my phone off of silent mode and begin to wipe my eyes so that I can see clearer.

And voice mails, text messages, and missed calls are all showing up on my screen—with the most recent call being only one minute ago from Indira.

"Rayci, have you or Sky talked to Indira?"

I ask her while interrupting her phone conversation now after seeing how many times Indira has called me.

"Yeah, I talked to her, but she knows not to say nothing to nobody outside of Rajon. I had to call and talk to her because Markus has been with Chris, and Adrian didn't answer. And I know that you and Sky are dealing with this just like I am, but she probably won't stop calling your phone until she can speak to you for herself."

"Shit!"

I shout as my phone begins to ring, and I look at it and see that it's Lamar.

"Just let it go to voice mail if you don't feel like talking to him right now."

Rayci now puts her phone back to her ear and says. "Hey, Momma, let me call you right back."

She now hangs up her phone and says to me.

"You're dealing with enough as it is, so Lamar is just going to have to wait until you can get yourself together before y'all can talk things out."

"I know, but he keeps calling me. So I'm going to have to answer him sooner or later to keep him from coming back out here. And if I could just stop crying so damn much, then maybe I'll be all right. I've never cried this hard before, not even when I saw my uncle get shot and he died right in front of me. And I don't know if it was because I was too angry to cry this much, or if I've really just taken on so much guilt that it has me feeling super bad about all of this. I mean I know that this was her own personal decision, but Rayci, this situation is really bothering me."

My phone begins to ring again, and my finger accidentally swipe to answer it as I wipe away my tears before I can even see who it is.

"Hey, baby!"

The male voice says on the other end of the receiver as I pause and put it to my ear, but I rush to hang it up.

"That was Lamar, damn! I should have been more careful! Look, he's calling again!"

"Give it to me!" She demands while reaching for my phone.

"Chad, will you come over here and talk to Lamar for Chase?" She says as soon as she sees him walking towards the door to go back into the cabin.

As he and Sky are headed back inside, and hopefully for a towel to wash Sky's face with because her face looks just as gloomy and puffy as mine.

"She don't know if she should tell Lamar about what's going on out here or not."

Rayci says. "But I'm thinking that if you tell him that the cops are here, then maybe he'll back off a little bit. And you can just explain to him what's all happened later, but he needs to know something so that he will quit calling her so much."

"I'll talk to him, but he's definitely going to want to know why the police are here if I bring it up, and I'll tell him. I just won't give him any details about anything, but I can talk to him and let him know that it's all bad out here right now."

Now turning to me, he says.

"But then he'll probably start back calling me to check on you until you can call him back for yourself."

"I'm going to call him, just not right now. But I'm definitely going to call him for sure."

"All right, well, give me the phone."

He says to Rayci just as my phone starts to ring again.

"Yo, what's up man? It's Chad."

He says to Lamar while walking away from us so that we can't hear their conversation.

But I now take in a deep breath and exhale in relief from the feeling of being free from having to explain anything to Lamar right now.

"Thanks Rayci. Girl, I didn't know how I was going to get out of having to talk to him."

"Chad was just about to go and ask the detectives what's going on because I told him that I'm ready to go home."

Sky interjects while rubbing the temples of her forehead.

"Me, too." Rayci and I both agree with her.

"But I can't leave until all of this has settled down, because I'm not leaving Markus out here by himself with Chris."

"I feel the same way, so I may end up just hanging around after I get this whole thing with Lamar under control. Because the police may need me for more questioning or whatever anyway, because I don't need to be suspected of any foul play due to our situation. So they can take all of the statements, pictures, and whatever else that they'll need to clear me of any wrong doing as far as what happened between us. I just hope that after Lamar hears about what happened, he'll back off. Because I want to stay out here in case Chris somehow needs me for anything as well. So Sky, if I can get him to back off, then you and Chad can go ahead and leave without me. And the rest of us can ride back in a rental car, or we'll just fly back, or whatever they choose."

"Here you go, Chase."

Chad comes back and gives me my phone.

"Damn, that was quick!"

I shout. "What did he say?"

"I think that Rayci was right when she said that we should tell Lamar something so that he'll stop calling you."

He says.

"But telling him the truth probably should have waited because he took the news about what Kris did in the same way as we all did. And he did say that he wouldn't come back out here after something like this has happened, but I don't believe him. Because he kept talking about how you and Kris were working on your relationship, and how he knows how much this is probably bothering you. He said that he will sit still until you can call him back. But like I said, I don't believe him. Especially after he kept talking about how much he wants to be here for you."

"So now what am I supposed to do?"

I question, then quickly come up with an answer on my own. "Don't even answer that because I know what I have to do, because as soon as he calls me back, I'm just going to tell him what's what and get it over with, period."

CHAPTER 24
"MORE BAD NEWS"

Markus comes over and informs us that Kris's mom will be pulling up any minute now.

"Chris said that he let Ms. Johnson speak to one of the detective's three hours ago when they first got here, and the detective told her enough to let her know that Kris is gone. Although he didn't actually say that she was deceased, but he said enough for her to know that she wasn't okay. And when Chris couldn't put Kris on the phone, no matter how many times she asked to speak to her. She knows for sure that something bad has happened, and since she lives only three hours away. She's almost here now."

"Oh wow, so we really do need to be getting Lamar on the phone to stop him from coming back out here for real now!" Sky says. "Because it's going to be a toxic situation if we have Kris's mom, Lamar, and Chris all out here together like that in front of these police. Chad, will you call Lamar and tell him that we're about to leave and come back home, so there's no need for him to come back this way for real. I'm sure that will stop him from coming back because he'll think that CJ is headed back that way."

Pulling his phone from his ear, Chad says. "This is my third time calling Lamar but he's not answering his phone. I've been calling him back to back ever since CJ said that she would just go ahead and tell him what's up."

"So Lamar is on his way back out here?" Markus asks.

"Not yet." Sky says.

"But we're trying to stop him before he does come back, so that there won't be any more craziness going on. And I bet he'll answer his phone if we call him back from CJ's number."

And although I said that I'm ready to talk to him, I hand my phone to Chad for him to call him back from my phone again. But for some reason Lamar still doesn't answer.

"Yeah, call him and tell him that everybody is about to pack and head back home. Because my brother is grieving right now, so it'll be another dead body coming up out here if he comes back on some bullshit. And I don't care if the police are out here or not, I'm going to make sure that he gets his issues dealt with by me personally."

Markus informs us of his intentions of handling this situation for his brother by any means necessary, and he isn't smiling or joking at all.

"See, that's what I'm talking about right there! We have to get him back on the phone so that he and CJ can talk because this is not cool!" Rayci says in a more serious tone as well, as if she already knows how much Markus means every word of what he's saying to us right now.

She says. "Chad, where was he when you talked to him?"

"I'm not sure where he was, but I'm thinking he was still at home, that's what I'm trying to find out."

Chad says. "But it does seem like he's under the impression that whatever he did is now forgotten, or just less important compared to what Kris did. But hopefully he won't try to come back after something like this for real."

"Here Chad. Will you call him again from my phone?"
I ask while handing him my phone once again.
"Man, this is the worst trip that I've ever been on in my life!"
Sky says. "And I'm so ready to go home that I don't even care
if we have to leave everything that we brought with us out here!
They can just mail me my stuff later!"
"I truly do feel where you're coming from with that—for real,
though."
Rayci says while now turning to Markus.
"Where's Chris?"
And before he can answer, we all see a car rapidly approaching
the cabin. And we watch Kris's mom, uncle, and sister get out
and come running towards us asking everybody what's
happened. And everybody; excluding me begins to explain.
And her mom and sister starts screaming and crying out to Kris,
but that's when one of the detectives comes to speak with them
about how their evidence shows how Kris had made sure that
nobody would be able to come inside of that room without
breaking into it like Chris did.
"We found a note, along with a few other things that indicates
that this was a suicide."
The detective says to them. "I'm so sorry for your loss."
"How long had she been hanging out there before they found
her?"
"That's what they're in there figuring out right now."
The detective now offers his condolences again.
"I'm sorry for your loss, ma'am."
And when Chris comes outside and sees everybody gathered
together as they're still trying to stop Ms. Johnson from going
inside, he rushes over to her as she cries out to him.
"What happened?"
She continues to cry out. "Why did she do this? I just can't
believe that she would do something like this! What happened?"

"I don't know!"

He says. "I knew that she was upset and everything, but not enough to leave me or little Chris like this!"

"She said that you told her that you couldn't be in a relationship with her anymore!"

Her sister Jackie, says. "So why is she even out here anyway? Were y'all trying to work it out or something? Because she told me that you were already looking for another place to stay and everything!"

Sobbing and continuing to cry, she hugs Ms. Johnson as they both release their sorrows and grieve together.

And now Kris's uncle asks Chris where is little Chris.

"He's with my auntie." Chris says. "Y'all know that my aunt Peggy won't let us take him nowhere else for a long period of time besides her house, so he's with her for the next few days."

"Yo, CJ, come here."

Chad interrupts my listening to them by coming over and getting in-between me and Sky.

"Why are you telling her to come here when you've already made it over here to us, Chad?" Sky asks while laughing.

"CJ, this is Lamar on the phone, and he wants to talk to you." He says with the phone held behind his back, while slickly gesturing for me and Sky to follow him over to the side of the cabin.

"How did you get him to answer his phone?" I ask him as we follow him to the side of the cabin.

"I didn't, he just called me from that gas station that's one exit away from here."

"What?" Sky and I both yell.

"Yep." He says. "He said that he's been on the highway during all of our calls, he just didn't want to tell me where he was."

"Fuck it, give me the phone and I'll tell him everything right now. Because this has gone on long enough."

I now take the phone from him as soon as we get completely around the corner, and without hesitation I confess.

"Lamar, you can't come back out here because I still don't want to be with you anymore. And I have feelings for someone else anyway, and I don't want any more trouble out here!"

But the phone is silent because the call has already been disconnected.

"Chad, there's nobody on this phone, he must have hung up before you gave me the phone."

"Well, let me call him back because he'll be here in about ten minutes if he's at that last gas station before the exit to come here. He told me that his phone went dead after we got off the phone earlier, but it's been on the charger so he didn't take it into the store with him. That's why he didn't answer, because he was in the store paying for his gas."

"I knew it!"

Sky shouts at us.

"I knew that this shit was going to happen!"

"A part of me knew this would happen, too. That's why I should have just gone ahead and told him last night, but I didn't know that he was already in route back out here."

"I'm trying to call him back."

Chad says. "But he either went back into the store, or his phone isn't getting a signal because he's not answering again."

"Fuck!"

I yell in frustration. "This is so fucked up!"

And now they both stand scratching their heads just as I am because I know how serious Markus is about handling this situation for Chris, just about as much as I know how much Lamar doesn't fear anybody, no matter who they are.

So after about five or six minutes of brainstorming.

Chad, Sky, and I finally decide that the three of us should start walking to meet Lamar down by the entrance of the cabin.

We decide that we should just walk far enough towards the entryway so that we can catch him before he makes it all the way here.

But sure enough, just as we are coming from around the corner, Lamar comes rapidly driving towards the cabin.

And now he gets out of the truck and comes walking towards everyone, while not only looking at us, but also at Chris and Markus.

CHAPTER 25
"LET'S GO HOME"

"Yo, Lamar, let me holler at you for a minute!" Chad says while quickly rushing over to him in a way that he's never done before, so Lamar looks at him with a weird look on his face.

"Wait!"

I stop him. "Chad, let me talk to him!"

"Talk to me about what?"

He says while looking at me and Chad like he can already tell that something isn't right.

"What's wrong?"

Lamar says. "I mean I know that a lot is wrong, but why do y'all look like that? Are you okay, Chase?"

"Actually, I'm not. So how about we go and talk in private over here by ourselves for a minute."

I now begin to walk faster towards him and in the direction of his truck. Thinking that the farther away we can get from the cabin, the better. But now Markus comes trotting in our direction like he's about to just go ahead and say or do whatever it is that he's going to say or do to cease the situation.

"Hold on, Lamar, let me talk to Markus for a minute to let him know that we're straight over here. Because you know that we can't have no drama going on out here in front of these police due to you trying to get back with me."

And my heart is beating so fast that it feels like it's about to come straight through my chest as I rush over to meet Markus.

"I don't know what's going on in your brain right now Markus, but let me deal with Lamar first before you say or do anything. Okay? Because the police are out here so nobody should be acting up, I promise you I can handle this."

"All right." He says calmly, and somewhat subtle.

"Go on and handle your business, but things have changed now CJ, y'all are not a couple."

"I know."

And as my heart continues to beat even faster now after walking away from him, I need to figure out a way to tell Lamar what I have to tell him without it causing too big of a scene.

"Baby, what's up?" Lamar says to me before I can even make it all the way back over to him.

"I heard about what Kris did, but something else seems to be going on right now."

"Okay Lamar, we really do need to talk because a lot has changed since you left."

I explain to him as we stand next to a big tree that's planted only a few feet away from the cabin's roadway.

"I know, there's a lot that we both need to talk about. And I'm going to let you say whatever it is that you want to say, but you gotta hear me out first this time, even though I may have blown it with you. You have to listen to me before we discuss anything, please, Chase. I'm not yelling or anything. I'm done, and I'll do whatever it is that I have to do to make this thing work between us, including changing the way that I make a living."

He says. "I promise I'll change whatever that needs to be changed to correct this whole thing. And I've never been so serious about making such a big change in my life, but I'm ready. I even had a talk with God on my way out here and promised him that if he allows you to give me another chance. Then I'll do whatever I have to do to show him, and you that you're the only woman for me. I'm sorry baby, just let me prove to you how much I love you and want to be with you and only you."

"That's not possible anymore, Lamar."

I now lower my head as I begin to speak my truth.

"That's what I'm trying to tell you. After you cheated on me with Tori, I did the same thing to you with Chris. And he's told me how much he loves me and wants to be with me and only me as well. And since your phone went dead, you didn't answer when I was trying to call to tell you not to come back out here because of that."

"What the fuck do you mean you did the same thing with Chris?"

He yells. "What happened with you and Chris?"

I now stand in silence and choose not to answer him right away, as I watch the veins in his neck grow, indicating how pissed he's getting.

But he still asks. "I said what the fuck happened between you and Chris?"

"You know what happened between me and Chris, don't make me spell it out for you! She sucked your dick, so I sucked his!"

And I immediately fall hard to the ground as blood begins to stream down my nose and into my mouth.

But I close my eyes and squeeze my head as hard as I can to try to stop the loud ringing sounds that are inside of my head as I hit the ground. I'm in so much shock that he's hauled off and hit me in front of everyone that I'm literally unable to move.

211

So needless to say that I don't fight back or anything.

I don't even know how many times he hit me in a matter of seconds, I just know that I feel like I just fell from a building head first into the dirt.

And as I now look up, I can vaguely see Chad damn near lifting Lamar completely off the ground to put him into his truck.

But things feel so much better if I keep my eyes closed and my head down, so all I can do mostly is hear Chad tussling with him by forcing him back into the truck.

And moments later, I know that they're inside the truck and speeding off like they're about to be involved in a high-speed chase.

And from what I can hear and see from the ground, it looks like one of the detectives has gotten into a vehicle and taken off behind them.

But I'm not fully sure of it because this pain is now on me real heavy, and I don't care about what they're doing anymore.

"Oh my God!"

Sky comes rushing over to me screaming, while Rayci, Chris, and Markus all rush over to me as well.

"I can't believe that he just did that!"

Sky rants on in anger.

"His ass is as good as got for this shit, oh my God! Look at your face!"

Chris now takes off his T-shirt and places it under my nose while I hold my head back to try to stop the blood flow. Thankfully Chad was the nearest to us and was able to get Lamar into that truck and away from here as quickly as he did. Although the pain in my head and face makes me feel like I not only fell from a building, but also like I was just involved in a head-on collision car crash. But it still doesn't stop me from noticing how Chris is continuously trying to get Markus to focus on me, instead of Lamar for right now.

Especially when he sees the woman detective running over to me, so now he's really doing all that he can to get Markus to calm down.

"Take her inside so that the medical professionals can take a look at her."

The detective says to them when she comes over and sees all of the blood on my face.

"And will somebody tell me what in the hell just happened out here?"

But Chris now picks me up to carry me inside.

"To be honest, I really don't feel comfortable being inside of this cabin anymore." I mumble as best as I can to them.

But I don't think anybody can hear me because the detective walks away from me to go and get help while Chris tells Sky, Rayci, and Markus that Lamar had better get the fuck out of the state today.

"He's going to die tomorrow if he doesn't disappear by tonight."

Chris says as we go into the cabin. "Apparently he's got me twisted or confused with someone else, or he just flat-out has a death wish in motion or something. I'm pissed, but I know that I can't really kill him this week without becoming a suspect after all that's happened, but he can still be kidnapped and never found again. But they'll probably lock him up for assault because his dumb ass did this shit right in front of the police. But baby brother, I guess we both need to calm down because this shit right here is about to send me into a place that I prefer not to go."

"Chris, please don't go to that place, okay?"

I mumble while still only talking to myself, because no one is paying me any attention as far as my muffled words.

"Will the both of you please stop talking like that out here, leave her here and just go back outside for some fresh air."

Rayci now tilts her head towards the door to alert them that the detective is now walking back over to us.

"Earlier they kept telling me that no one is allowed inside of this cabin. But now since everyone has been walking in and out of here, I hope that it's okay that I stay in here, too."

Rayci says to the detective while looking around like they are about to say something to her.

"I'm not going anywhere near that room so maybe you guys will let me stay."

"You're fine."

The detective informs her while moving to the side to let the medical worker tend to me.

"We were only telling you that earlier because we were in the middle of trying to figure out what happened, and we couldn't chance anything being tampered with after our arrival. But we're almost done now so you're okay."

She says. "Now, Ms. Jordan, can you explain to me what just happened out there? And who all was in the vehicle that sped away?"

"I'm sorry, Detective. But the more I talk, the worse my face feels. So can you give me a moment before I have to answer any questions?"

I mumble as best as I can, while she comes closer to my face so that she can hear what I'm saying after having to repeat myself.

"Sure."

She says. "I'm sorry, I should wait until after you've been looked at anyway."

"Your nose is definitely broken."

The medical worker now says to me.

"You're going to have to go to the hospital to get this taken care of, along with this cut over your eye."

"He just went outside, but I'll go and get Markus and tell him that I have to leave and go to the hospital with you."

"Wait." I mutter to stop Rayci from going to get him, as I'm stricken with pain every time my face moves.

But I don't care because like Sky, I'm now ready to get back home whether Chris stays out here or not at this point.

"I don't want to go to the hospital out here."

I stress to them all. "But I will go straight to the hospital as soon as we get back to the city. So can you just give me something for this pain since it's going to take us four hours to get to the hospital near my house?"

"I can only give you as much pain medicine as I'm allowed to give you until we can get you to a local hospital, and they can administer more. And the swelling is coming, so I recommend that you go to the hospital that's only fifteen minutes away from here."

And now the detective chimes in and says.

"I was just told that we now have the person who assaulted you, so you should definitely go to the nearest hospital for treatment. And I need to get a little more information from you about Ms. Johnson, as well as more information about this incident."

And as Sky is now standing next to us, and has listened to the medical worker and the detective. She says. "CJ, Chris told me to check to see if there are any flights available so that none of us will have to drive home. But I didn't see any decent departing flights, so he said that he was about to call his friends from Evans and Goldstein. Because they owe him a favor, and after all that's happened, he's about to use that favor by getting their private plane to take us back home. Since every airline that I called can either take only one of us, or there's a long layover or something, because none of them has anything for today or in the morning that will fly us all the way home without stopping. And he said that he's going to stay out here with Ms. Johnson and help with Kris, so he's out there right now checking to see if they can get clearance for us to use their plane."

"Oh that's good."

Rayci says. "And I'm sure that Markus will be staying here with Chris, so I'll go with her to the hospital if we have time to go before the flight leaves. Because taking that pain for four hours just wasn't going to work anyway, I'm sad and ready to get back home as well, but that just wasn't going to work."

"What did you find out Chris?"

Sky asks while Chris now comes back inside while walking towards us.

"Yeah."

Rayci says. "What did you find out because CJ doesn't want to go to the hospital out here? But I told her that waiting four hours to be treated will be too much."

"Why?"

He says while kneeling down to where I am.

"CJ, you definitely need to go to the hospital out here. And my friends are going to let the three of you fly back on their jet, and I'll stay here until things are figured out. But go to the hospital Chase, because they said that y'all will have to wait almost two hours before y'all can leave anyway. So go and get taken care of, and the police have Lamar, so you don't have to worry about him coming to find you."

He says. "The detective said that Chad said that he went to the entrance of the cabin and waited because he knew that they would follow him, but he wanted to get Lamar out of sight to avoid any more violence or whatever. So he told him that he wasn't fleeing the police, that's why he pulled over and was waiting for them. He fled the scene because he was trying to help the situation, so let's continue to help the situation by getting you taken care of right now. Because I really need to focus on Ms. Johnson, and even myself at this point. And we need to make sure that the hospital and the police have all the information that they need before you leave."

"I agree."
The detective says. "That's why you need to go to the local hospital so that you can get some relief, you'll still be able to make your flight if you choose to get most of your treatment at home. Although I'm not sure how much medicine they'll give you at the hospital, but I'm sure that it'll be more than you're able to get here. Especially since you'll be in pain after answering my questions, so are you okay to leave now?"
"Yes."
I answer. "I would like to finish this at the hospital."
"Okay, I'll be right back."
Now my only concern other than this pain is that this detective is going to think that I'm able to answer her questions now since I'm speaking as much as I am, but I'm really not in the mood or in good shape to keep talking so much.
"So do I need to get the guys from the security house to help you all pack?"
Chris asks while trying to do whatever he can to get this taken care of. Although dealing with us, Ms. Johnson, and everyone else has to be overwhelming for him.
But I guess he's just doing whatever he feels that he has to do.
"No."
Rayci says to Chris. "You don't have to get anyone to help us because I'll pack our things and CJ's."
"I was going to pack our things and CJ's, too."
Sky says. "But who will go with her to the hospital if we have to stay here and be packed and ready in two hours?"
Sky continues. "I don't mind if the guys from the security house pack for us, so I'll go with CJ while y'all stay here if that's cool."
"It's cool with me." Rayci says. "They can just help me pack each room. I won't go into Chris' room, but I'll make sure that everything else is packed and ready to go."

"Okay."

Sky says as she's about to leave to go and get her purse, and whatever else that she'll need because I'm sure that she'll be on her phone making sure that Chad is okay after we leave.

Although Chris is now telling her that the detective said that Chad will be fine, they're just talking to him more about what all happened.

Along with him telling her that Chad said that he wants to stay out here with him and Markus.

Rayci and Sky now leave us to go and get prepared to leave, just as the detective and the medical worker has done.

And with this brief moment of being alone, Chris says. "Baby, I know how bad this is, but you know that I'm about to have my hands full with Ms. Johnson and Kris' family members. But Jackie knows more about our relationship than Ms. Johnson does, so she's out there trying to explain how Kris just didn't take it well that we were splitting. And I'm glad that she was talking to Jackie about us so much because with the note that she left, along with the things that she's been saying to Jackie. They can see how much our separating affected her, and Jackie said that Kris called her and left a message last night. But she didn't see or hear the message until this morning, so she's beating herself up because she feels like she wasn't there for her in her time of need. And since she's not mad at me, I'm trying to stay close to her because Jackie knew how much I was done with our relationship. Because she said that she told Kris that you can't force someone to be with you if they don't want to be with you anymore, so she was trying to encourage her to move on. But Kris wouldn't listen to her, so I'm just trying to be here for them because it's my job to be here. And I really am glad that she talked so much because they're not blaming me for this shit due to what she's been saying recently. But I'm not going home until we can take Kris back with us."

He says quickly before anyone comes back. "But baby go and get treated and then go home and make sure that you don't have any communication with Lamar. And keep your eyes open just in case he just so happen to have someone to call you for him, because you know that he's bold enough to do it. Unless this news sticks to him like it did with Kris, and he no longer wants to talk because he'll only be thinking about revenge."

"I understand."

I say as best as I can.

"Don't worry about me because I'm going to be okay. Go and do what you need to do, and just call me if you need me. I'll keep my phone near me at all times, and after you get us more flight information. I'll still call or text you before we board the jet to go home. And me communicating with Lamar directly, or through someone else is not even an option anymore, so don't worry about that either."

Sky now comes back holding her phone and her cute designer bag in her hand. She says. "Chris, make sure that y'all call me the minute they're done with Chad, so that I can talk to him again."

"Okay."

He now places his attention back to me, but right as he's about to say something. Sky says. "Wait, CJ, what do you need for me to grab for you?"

"Just my purse and some sweat pants."

"Okay." She says while turning around to go and get it.

"I'm sure that they're going to try to keep you at the hospital, or try to set you up for surgery or something since your nose is broken. But since you're refusing to stay for full treatment, I don't know how all of that stuff works. But whenever you do leave the hospital, don't go home. I'll have Chauncey stay with you at a hotel until I can come back home."

"That's unnecessary, but I get why it needs to happen so okay, if that's what you want then I'll do it. I'm not going to let my girls know that our trip has been cut short anyway, so I'll stay wherever I need to stay for safety and privacy because it's just me for the next few days."

Soon, Sky comes back with my purse, some sweat pants for me to put on top of my pajama pants, and a t-shirt.

And while Chris leaves me to go and be with Kris' family.

Sky helps me to get dressed as we prepare to leave and never return.

And at this point, I'm thinking after we land back at home, I will go to the hospital without letting not just my daughter's.

But I won't let anyone know that our trip has been cut short because who knows what all is about to happen when we get back now that things have changed so much.

And I especially don't want my girls anywhere around while I try to get things under some kind of control, but getting back to my comfort zone in my own zip code is what I think is best for me right now.

Although Chris and I will definitely have to sit down and have a serious talk with just the five of us present and unmovable until we're all clear about where we all stand as a family unit, and as individuals.

Even though little Chris is too young to understand any of it, my children loves little Chris and big Chris like they love their own dad and Lamar. So a lot will have to be discussed and changed in order for us to make sure that we're all safe and clear about what's what from this day forward.

MEKO

VOLUME 2

Chasing Reality

CHAPTER 1
"A FRESH START"

There's no place like home holds true to its meaning as I lay my head back and onto my own pillow for the first time in weeks.

I've been relaxing in a hotel recovering from rhinoplasty after needing my nose fixed after Lamar had broken it.

"That hotel was so big and luxurious, and I'm so happy to have this new house and all of this new furniture! But I could just kiss you for making sure that my pillows and my favorite blanket was not replaced!"

I commend with happiness flowing through my body. "Everything around me can be luxurious and brand-new, but these pillows and this blanket really makes me feel good and right back at home again!"

"Chris was about to give the blanket and pillows away Momma, until I told him that you would've had a fit."

Leeyah says. "But Adrian and I made sure that we kept an eye on everything that we know that you love, and we made sure that it was properly packed."

"Well, thanks love."
I say while smiling and squeezing my blanket.
"I appreciate that."
"You're welcome, and we knew that you would appreciate it."
Chris came to me while I was in the hospital and explained to me how no one has been able to find Lamar since the violent incident at the cabin.
And that does bother me because Lamar doesn't hide from anyone, and since he made bail after assaulting me. Not only can the police not find him, but Chris nor any of his crew can find him either.
So I really can't stop thinking that he's just somewhere waiting for me to appear, so that he can finish what he started when he touched me with his fist.
Because now that Chris and I live together, and are really a couple. I feel like he's somewhere waiting with vengeance, hatred, and disrespect in his heart.
So I won't be truly satisfied until he's found because I know that he's feeling scorned and ready for whatever.
But after the passing of Kris, and now everybody knowing how Chris and I feel about each other. He asked if we can all live together under one roof because he didn't want to have to deal with everything by himself.
And since they can't find Lamar, he also wants us all together until they do. And since my house only has three bedrooms, I told him that I could just rent it out to someone while he and I build a house together, or for now just buy this beautiful five-bedroom house until we can figure everything else out.
"Guess who it is!"
Adrian now comes bursting into the room with me and Leeyah.
"Hey Boo!" I hail with excitement. "Girl, I owe you big-time for going to my office and helping out with everything since I've been missing in action!"

"It was no problem at all, CJ, your staff is so professional and have everything running so smoothly that I really didn't have to do all that much."

"Well, I still want to say thank you for going down there and making sure that everything was okay. You know that Sky had to fly out of town for a few days, while Chris has his own businesses to run."

"Chris had somebody else running his businesses because all he was running was us!"

She says while laughing.

"Girl, he was bossing us around and trying his best to get this place perfect for you!"

Adrian continues with a smile on her face.

"But I have to give it to him though, he really is trying to make you as happy as he can."

"I know, and that's why I cried and prayed so much last night after thinking about how everything that has happened, somehow seems to have purposely led us to this point. And I don't feel guilty anymore when I say that I'm happy, because all I did was fall in love with a man who has fallen in love with me."

"So you done got yourself a new nose and now you don't know how to call nobody?"

Indira interrupts us as she and Rayci now all of a sudden comes walking through the door.

"Oh my God, what is this—a reunion?"

I shout while laughing and getting up to give everybody a big hug.

Because Adrian is right, Chris has been doing everything that he can to try to make sure that I'm happy.

So he's been having them to help him get everything situated while requesting that I be left alone to physically heal and to mentally deal with everything thus far.

And I must say that I'm happy that he did that because we've all had the chance to really miss each other, after only communicating through phone calls and text messages every now and then for almost two months.

So now that I feel a thousand times better, we can all use this time to reconnect and catch up on what's been going on in our lives.

Thank you for reading!

Be sure to order, *Chasing* Reality, Volume 2 of *"The Chase Series"* to find out how Chase is highly mistaken when she gets too comfortable after settling into her new life.
When in reality, her old life has not quite ended, and she may be forced to face her old transgressions completely on her own.

And for more fiction and non-fiction books written by Meko, please visit her online at www.eaglelifepublications.net.

Let's Connect! Please follow Meko, and be sure to leave a review!

MEKO

www.ingramcontent.com/pod-product-compliance
Lightning Source LLC
Chambersburg PA
CBHW060430180626
46817CB00007B/2751